ROMILA

Indian Tales

Illustrated by
ABU ABRAHAM

PUFFIN BOOKS

PUFFIN BOOKS

Penguin Books India (P) Ltd., 11 Community Centre, Panchsheel Park,
New Delhi- 110 017, India
Penguin Books Ltd., 27 Wrights Lane, London W 8 5 TZ, UK
Penguin Books USA Inc., 375 Hudson Street, New York, NY- 10014, USA
Penguin Books Australia Ltd., Ringwood, Victoria, Australia
Penguin Books Canada Ltd., 10 Alcorn Avenue, Suite 300, Toronto
Ontario, M 4 V 3 B 2, Canada
Penguin Books (NZ) Ltd., 182-190 Wairau Road, Auckland 10, New Zealand

First published by Penguin Books India (P) Ltd. 1991

10 9 8 7 6 5

Copyright © Romila Thapar 1991

Typeset in Palatino by Interpress Magazines Pvt. Ltd., New Delhi.
Made in India by Ananda Offset Pvt. Ltd. Calcutta

This time round the book is for
Tahira, Jaisal, Shirin
Dhiraj, Ya-feng
Aditi and Savera

CONTENTS

CONTENTS

PREFACE

Many years ago I had given a lecture for children at the Victoria and Albert Museum in London on some myths and legends depicted in Indian art. Out of this lecture arose a collection of stories which I wrote for children and which were published as *Indian Tales*. The present book has retained many of those stories, only omitting a few which seemed to me to be too well-known to bear repetition.

This collection does not conform to any particular type of story; myths, folk-tales, fables and legends woven around historical characters, have all been included. My purpose has been to retell some of the stories with which I grew up, irrespective of the source or category.

Some are taken from mythology and are narrated as I remember them from many years ago. Another story comes from the *Mahabharata*, which has a vast number of stories slotted into the main narrative. I have retold one of these, 'Nala and Damayanti'. Such stories are often about heroes and heroines, their adventures, misfortunes and triumphs.

Stories with which children grow up are frequently distilled from formal collections, the process of retelling bringing about changes in the story. Such formal collections of stories in India go back to early times. Among these were the *Jataka* stories which linked character and event to Buddhist ethics.

Fables were also known in India at a very early date. They were generally animal stories with a moral which was revealed in the course of the story. Among the more popular were those included in the collection known as the *Panchatantra*. Later collections of stories included those in the *Kathasaritasagara* and the *Kathakosha*.

Associated with fables and sometimes similar in form are folk tales, but these can also be just stories without a moral. It is difficult to choose among these as they are so plentiful, but often the same idea is repeated in different versions. The ones I have selected come from various parts of the Indian sub-continent.

India is rich in stories associated with historical personalities. But after each generation of story-tellers has modified or added to the original story, it can hardly be called historical. Sometimes we do not know who is being referred to in the story, as in the case of 'The Throne of King Vikram'. In other stories the narrative is more interesting than the personality, as in 'How Birbal saved his Life'. And sometimes a romantic story enhances a historical person, such as in the story of 'Baz Bahadur and Rupamati'.

In giving the textual sources for a few of the stories it is not my intention to suggest that my version of the story follows the text closely. The retelling is largely from memory. I have therefore, in such cases, kept broadly to the main narrative, but have not hesitated to make changes where the mood has moved me.

I am more than delighted with the association of two friends of long standing with this book. Abu has once again done the illustrations for the stories and Amena Jayal, the cover.

New Delhi
1991   Romila Thapar

The Churning of the Milk Ocean

There was once a rishi who was renowned for his wisdom and knowledge. He had spent many years in meditation. There was no subject on which he could not speak with knowledge, so each time that the kings of the earth held a gathering, they invited him. His advice was always very welcome. On his way home from one such occasion he was presented with a garland of flowers picked from the trees in heaven. Instead of going home directly, the sage thought he would call on the gods. Then, as the garland was in his hands, he decided to make a present of it to Indra, who he thought was the most suitable god to receive it.

Indra welcomed the sage with much affection. Even the gods admitted that the sage was indeed very wise and were respectful towards him. But later, not knowing what to do with the garland, Indra tossed it over to his favourite elephant Airavata, standing nearby. The elephant was delighted. He kept throwing the garland up into the air and catching it on his trunk. The sage saw this. He was furious at the lack of respect by Indra. 'How dare he. I honour him by presenting him with a garland which had been given to me and he has the cheek to give it as a plaything to his elephant,' he thought. In his anger, he cursed not only Indra but all the gods. 'May they all lose their strength and become as weak as mortals.' Having done this he returned home, still seething with anger.

Soon after, the demons attacked the gods in their heavenly city and war was declared between them. It went on for many months. Whereas previously the gods would have been able to defeat the demons fairly easily, they now found it difficult to do so, as they had lost their strength because of the curse of the sage. As time went on they began to fear that they would be defeated by the demons. So they held a meeting. They decided that they would appeal to Brahma for help. They went to him and asked him what they should do. But Brahma could not help them. The curse of the sage was too powerful. So they went to Shiva. But he too could not help. Finally, they went to Vishnu, the third of the three great gods. Vishnu was asleep. The gods started singing hymns in his praise, gradually increasing the volume of their voices till eventually, Vishnu woke up. They explained to him why they had come to see him. At first Vishnu said that he too was powerless to help but then he thought for a while. 'There is only one way out of this,' he said. 'You must all drink a drop of nectar. That will give you greater strength than you have ever had.'

'Where can we find the nectar?' enquired Indra.

'You must churn the vast ocean of milk, one of the seven oceans which surround the earth, and it will emerge from the depths,' replied Vishnu, and having told them that he went to sleep again.

The gods now faced the problem of how they were going to churn the ocean of milk. To start with they would require a really strong and firm churning-stick. One of them suggested that they should uproot the tallest mountain Mandara, a suggestion that was agreed upon. But the next problem was, that the gods alone were not strong enough to lift the mountain. Again an assembly was called. This time it was suggested that the demons should be invited to help in the churning of the milk ocean. Some of the gods objected to this, and said, quite rightly, that the demons would never agree unless they too could drink the nectar. 'If this happened, then the demons would still be stronger than us,' a small group of gods protested. Whilst they were debating this point, Vishnu once more appeared on the scene, and said, that the gods should go ahead and make the offer to the demons and that the rest would somehow be managed by him.

The offer was made and the demons eagerly accepted it. War was halted while both forces joined together and prepared for the churning of the ocean of milk. The mountain Mandara was uprooted and was brought slowly and placed in the centre of the milk-ocean. Then they needed a sufficiently long rope. This problem was solved by the suggestion that the mighty snake, Vasuki, be used. Vasuki was twisted around the mountain, thus forming a churning rope.

Soon all was ready for the churning. There was much gaiety and excitement at the thought that the nectar would bestow immortality on all who drank it. A small difference of opinion arose as to which side should hold which end of the serpent. The gods wished to hold the end with the head but the demons refused to hold the end with the tail. The gods gave in and this was lucky for them for, as the churning became faster, the serpent breathed out fumes that weakened the demons. But this was not all. Soon there was another bigger problem. The bed of the ocean, being made of soft mud, could not hold the weight of the mountain. As the churning quickened, the gods and the demons were horrified to see that the mountain began to slowly sink into the mud. Vishnu was quick to notice this and he immediately turned himself into a giant tortoise. He swam down to the depths and placed himself under the mountain. The shell of the tortoise being very firm, the mountain was now supported by a solid foundation.

The churning made such a stir in the ocean, that various things which had for long lain at the bottom, floated up to the top. Among these were many precious objects with magical qualities. There came the moon, a parijata tree with its fragrant blossoms, the wish-fulfilling cow, the goddess of wine, the apsaras or nymphs, the goddess of prosperity seated on a full blown lotus, a conch shell, a mace and a jewel. All these things were grabbed by various gods. The poison which rose up was swallowed by Shiva so it could do no harm. At last, when the gods and the demons were exhausted, there arose the form of a physician who held in his hand, the bowl containing nectar.

Each one rushed towards the bowl. There was much pushing and jostling between them. In the end, the demons grabbed the bowl and made off with it. The gods were upset and terrified. Not only was there little likelihood of the demons sharing the nectar with them, but the demons would now be twice as strong. The demons meanwhile, started fighting over who should have the first sip.

Vishnu, seeing what was happening, was quick to act. The demons suddenly saw in their midst, an extremely beautiful young woman. She was dressed in the finest of clothes with exquisite jewels. As she looked at them shyly, the demons almost forgot about the nectar. One of them shouted, ' Here is the solution to our problem. We have been fighting over who is to have the first sip of the nectar. Let us offer it to this wonderful creature that stands in our midst and ask her to divide it between us.' They wrongly assumed that she was theirs to command.

The young woman (who was in reality, Vishnu in disguise) made the gods and the demons sit in two rows on either side of her. She explained that since they had both put an equal effort into the churning, the nectar must be fairly shared. She then took the bowl to the gods first, assuring the demons that she would see to it that there would be more than enough left for them. Each god took a sip. When she had completed offering it to the gods, the young woman vanished along with the nectar.

The demons were wild with anger. They realized that the gods had played a trick on them and started attacking them. A fierce battle took place, with the demons wielding every weapon in their power in an effort to crush the gods. But the gods had drunk the nectar and were now so full of strength that the blows of the demons felt like the touch of feathers. This enraged the demons even more. Through their own stupidity they had not only lost the nectar but also the possibility of ever defeating the gods. Badly beaten, they returned home.

It so happened that one amongst the demons had been able to sip the nectar. He had managed to pass himself off as a god by seating himself in their row. As he had taken a sip, the Sun and the Moon god, who were sitting on either side of him, discovered that he was, in fact, a demon. In their effort to kill him, they cut off his head. But the nectar had already taken effect and the head had become immortal. The story has it that it was placed amidst the planets and is called Rahu.

Rahu never forgave the Sun and the Moon gods for recognizing who he was and trying to kill him. Even to this day, from time to time Rahu attempts to swallow the sun or the moon. That is why, according to mythology, we have eclipses.

Nala and Damayanti

Nala was the young ruler of Nishada and a tiger among men. Although he was young, he had the wisdom of an experienced ruler. He was just in his decisions and was surrounded by people who were hard-working and intelligent. Nala was also a keen huntsman and an excellent archer. He enjoyed poetry and would often compose poems. Of all his pastimes, he spent the most number of hours driving chariots. His handling of horses was unsurpassed in the land. Even the men whose profession it was to drive chariots had to agree that Nala was better than any of them. There was only one thing that Nala lacked: a queen who would be his equal.

People began to wonder which of the eligible young women would please him and to whom he would be acceptable. She had to be beautiful but above all she would also have to be intelligent and able to enjoy the pleasures of music and poetry. Various princesses were mentioned, but in each there was some fault. Finally, it seemed that there was only one who was fault-less and she was Damayanti, the daughter of the king of Vidarbha. Her fame had begun to spread to distant places. The wandering minstrels who travelled from court to court would sing songs in her praise. It was thus that Nala came to hear of her, and her image, described by the minstrels, stayed in his mind. Damayanti too had heard of the deeds of Nala from the minstrels and from those at her father's court who were always talking about the remarkable Nala. And thus, although they had never met, Nala and Damayanti developed a mutual fondness and decided individually that they would marry only each other.

One day Nala was wandering alone in his garden when a flock of geese flew past him. They were so close that he stretched out his hands and caught one of them. The terrified bird said to Nala, 'Do not hurt me, great hero. If you let me go free, I will do you a favour in return. I shall go directly to Damayanti and tell her of your love for her.' Nala released the bird and let it fly away. The bird flew straight to the garden were Damayanti and her friends were strolling. It flew round them in circles. The girls were delighted and tried to catch it. However the bird kept flying out of their reach and soon they were tired, except Damayanti, who continued to give chase. The bird, seeing that Damayanti's friends were now at some distance, alighted and said softly, 'I have come to tell you that Nala, the king of Nishada, is the man you must marry. He has great qualities and you alone are suited to him.' Damayanti was startled at first by these words. The goose had said aloud what she had been wishing for. Damayanti sighed and answered, 'Please, dear bird, speak to him in the same way about me.' The goose flew away, and Damayanti returned to her friends, more thoughtful than before.

The weeks passed by. Nala and Damayanti kept thinking of each other and wondering how they would eventually manage to marry. Meanwhile Damayanti's parents decided that it was time to find her a husband. So they asked her if she was willing to have a svayamvara. This was a ceremony which all the eligible princes from far and near would attend for the princess to choose her husband. Damayanti was delighted to hear this. She had, of course, made up her mind that she would choose Nala. So she readily agreed to the svayamvara.

The proclamation was made. Messengers were sent out in all directions with invitations to the various princes. On a certain day, they would all assemble in the palace of Damayanti's father. Since Damayanti's fame had already travelled far and wide, there were many princes who were eager to marry her. Even the gods in heaven, when they heard that she was holding a svayamvara, thought they would go along and present themselves. Of these, the four gods Indra, Agni, Varuna and Yama began to make preparations. They were the gods of War, of Fire, of the Waters and of Death, respectively.

The day before the ceremony was to be held, the roads leading to the capital were crowded with the chariots, the palanquins and the baggage of the various princes who had come for the ceremony. Nala was there too, hardly able to calm his excitement at the thought that he was at last going to see Damayanti and, if all went well, to wed her.

Travelling along the same road as Nala were the four gods. They knew about the love Nala and Damayanti shared but they wanted to test them. So they approached Nala, and said, 'Greetings to you, Nala. It seems that you too are going to the svayamvara. We want a trustworthy messenger to take a message for us. Will you promise to do so?' Nala agreed and then asked them who they were. Indra introduced them, and added, 'We are all four going to present ourselves at the svayamvara tomorrow. We want you to go to Damayanti and tell her that the gods will be there and that she must choose one of them for her husband.'

Nala was most dejected when he heard this. He pleaded: 'Please spare me this torture, I implore you. How can I deliver this message? I too am hoping to wed Damayanti, and, what is more, we have already vowed that we shall marry no one but each other.' The gods were angry at this. 'Why did you promise then to deliver the message at first?' said Indra. 'If you don't do so now, you will be breaking your promise.' Sadly, Nala asked, 'How can I enter Damayanti's room in the palace? The palace servants will never let me through. I am a stranger to them.' 'Never mind,' replied Indra. 'We can arrange that.'

He had hardly finished speaking when Nala found himself in Damayanti's room. The princess was seated in a far corner, laughing and talking to a group of friends. There was much activity in the room, with maids coming and going and preparations being made for the ceremony. Some were bringing in clothes and cosmetics, others were stringing flowers for garlands while still others were mixing perfumes. At times somebody would come rushing in with news and a description of the latest prince to arrive. Nala watched all this unseen for a few moments. But his eyes kept returning to Damayanti. He could hardly believe that he was seeing her at last. But the sad reality of why he had come, cut short his dreaming and he stepped forward to speak to her. There was a sudden hush in the room, for the girls were struck by the bearing of the handsome stranger who was suddenly in their midst. He looked so young and yet so sad. Nala went straight up to Damayanti. She waved her friends away, and turning to him asked, 'Who are you, gentle stranger, and how did you manage to come here without being stopped by the palace servants?'

'I am Nala,' he replied simply, and as Damayanti looked at him in astonishment, he hastened to add, 'I have come here through the power of the gods, unseen by the palace servants. I bring you a message from them. The gods Indra, Agni, Varuna and Yama will be at the ceremony tomorrow. They have asked me to tell you that you must choose one of them for your husband.' Damayanti was taken aback. 'But I have decided to marry you, Nala, and I cannot choose one of the gods.' She was in tears and Nala felt helpless. Then suddenly she said, 'I know what I shall do, and this will not in any way harm you. Tell the gods that you have delivered their message to me but that I shall choose you from among the entire assembly tomorrow.'

The day arrived when all the princes and kings assembled for the ceremony. The large audience hall in the palace shone with the splendour of the preparations. Its polished floor and pillars reflected the colour of the hangings on the walls and the banners. The princes were seated around the hall, each with a small group of friends and attendants. The room echoed with the murmur of voices as the excitement mounted. Heralds would rush from one group to another making last minute enquiries. Some of the contestants smiled encouragement and others glowered at each other. Nala found to his surprise that the four gods were seated on either side of him.

In the midst of the noise and the hubbub, a loud announcement was made, which brought silence into the assembly. Damayanti entered the hall. The people gathered there were taken aback. They had heard of her beauty from the minstrels and the bards. But she was far lovelier than they had expected. She had everything that a poet could praise—a round face like the full moon, eyes shaped like lotus buds with eyebrows that arched firmly above them, a well-set nose, a small mouth, a glowing dark skin and black hair. Slim-waisted, she moved with ease and grace. Damayanti carried a large garland and she walked up to where her parents sat. As she walked, a thousand pairs of eyes followed her every movement. She bowed low before her father and mother, who blessed her. She was then conducted from group to group, whilst a minstrel proclaimed the qualities of each prince. There was a hush in the hall, broken only from time to time by the sound of the minstrel's voice and the gentle tinkle of the anklets on Damayanti's feet. The princes waited in fearful excitement, their hearts beating wildly. But Damayanti was calm. She walked with her eyes lowered and knew that as soon as she came to where Nala was seated she would place the garland round his neck and thus declare her choice.

At last she reached Nala. She looked up to catch a brief glimpse of his face before garlanding him. But when she looked up she saw five princes, each identical, each one the image of Nala. Which of these five was her Nala? She realized that the gods had played a trick on her and that it would be impossible for her to distinguish who the real Nala was. Silently she prayed to the gods to forgive her for choosing a mortal instead of a god.

The gods, seeing that nothing would make her change her mind, took pity on her and revealed themselves. Damayanti noticed that of the five, only the one in the centre was blinking his eyes. He alone cast a shadow in the light, the flowers in his garlands had begun to fade and there were traces of dust and sweat on him. Above all, his feet were touching the ground, whereas those of the other four were not. She recognized the signs of immortals and knew that the figure in the centre was Nala. So she placed her garland round his neck, amidst the congratulations of those who were there. Her troubles seemed to be over. They were finally married.

After the ceremony the princes departed, each to his own kingdom. The four gods, Indra, Agni, Varuna and Yama, started on their journey home. On the way they met two of the gods of Time—of the Dvapara age and of the Kali age—also known sometimes as the god of Twilight and the god of Darkness. 'Where are you going?' asked Indra. 'To the svayamvara of Damayanti,' replied Kali. 'I wish to marry her.' Indra laughed and told him that he was too late since Damayanti had already married Nala. 'What?' said Kali in astonishment, 'has she dared to choose a mortal when the gods themselves were competing for her? She must be punished for this.' The other four gods tried to pacify him. They explained what had happened and how they had permitted her to choose Nala. 'Besides,' added Indra, 'the mortal she has chosen is almost a god, so fine a man is he.' But the god of Darkness was not to be comforted, and he went his way, muttering and mumbling that he would see Damayanti humbled.

Twelve years passed. Nala and Damayanti were living in great happiness together with their two children, a son and daughter. But Kali was still hovering around, waiting to take his revenge on them. Finally, he succeeded. He entered the mind of Nala and made him act in a strange way. Nala's brother challenged him to a game of dice and Nala agreed to play. Not knowing anything about dice, he kept losing. Damayanti and his friends begged him to stop playing but he took the game very seriously and continued. They could not understand what had come over him. He had never behaved like this in the past. They did not know, of course, that it was Kali who had possessed him and who was urging him on.

Nala and his brother began to play for high stakes. Nala continued to lose—first his jewels and ornaments, then the palace and soon after, the kingdom itself. He was finally left only with his wife and two children. Damayanti, not knowing what Nala would do next, asked one of her friends to take the two children to the home of her parents where they would be safe. Nala's brother now suggested that they play a game of dice with Damayanti as the stake. But by this time Nala had begun to realize that he had lost everything so he decided to leave. Full of shame, he suggested that Damayanti also join her parents where she would be more comfortable but she refused and insisted that she would be with Nala wherever he went. So the two set out, with the clothes they were wearing as their sole possessions.

They wandered through the forest, foot-sore, tired and hungry. They had only the berries from the trees to eat. Nala kept insisting that Damayanti should go home to her parents as life with him would now be harsh and uncomfortable. But she would not part from him. One day, Nala saw a pair of large yellow birds pecking at worms on the ground. Thinking that they would be just right for a meal, he carefully unwound the cloth he was wearing and threw it over them, in an attempt to catch them. The birds flew up into the air, carrying the cloth with them. Nala had now lost everything. He was forced to share his wife's clothes.

They roamed through the forest for some days until they arrived at a small, sheltered place where travellers occasionally rested. They lay down to sleep. However, Nala was restless.

After a great deal of thinking, he got up silently and walked alone deeper into the forest. He felt sure that Damayanti, on waking up and not seeing him there, would eventually find her way back to her father's palace, and thereby lead a more comfortable life. This was a terrible decision for Nala as he did not really want to part from her. But since it was his fault that she had to roam through the forest, he felt it was better to leave her and thus force her to go back.

A few years passed by. Damayanti had searched everywhere for Nala, and not finding him, decided to return to her parents' home. Her life was sad. She thought of Nala all the time and wondered what had happened to him. Meanwhile, Nala, who had wandered into the depths of the forest, had started thinking of how he could win back his kingdom. In the course of his wanderings, he suddenly saw a huge forest fire and as he approached it, a voice cried out, 'Nala, I need your help. Step into the fire. Don't be frightened.' Nala did as he was told. He saw a large snake coiled up at the centre of the flames. The snake spoke: 'I am under a curse. Only you can save me. Please lift me up and take me to a particular place to which I shall direct you. Don't be afraid.' Nala wondered how he would ever be able to lift such a large creature but as he put out his arms to lift it, it turned into a tiny snake, so small that Nala could carry it in the palm of one hand.

He carried it to the place as directed. As he was about to put it down on the ground, the snake bit him. Immediately, Nala felt himself shrink a little. His skin became rough and his hands looked gnarled. The snake, seeing Nala's bewilderment, said, 'Don't be anxious about yourself, Nala. I bit you so that the poison will enter Kali who has possessed you. I have also given you a new form so that no one may recognize you. But you will return to your normal self as soon as you have done what you wish to do. If you want to win back your kingdom and live with your wife in happiness once more, then do as I say. Go to the king of Ayodhya. He will employ you as a charioteer. He is very skilled in playing with dice. Learn from him and challenge your brother. When you have done so and wish to get back your original form, wear these two garments which I am giving you and concentrate your thoughts on me.' With these words, the snake vanished. Nala was left standing with two garments in his hand, more puzzled than before.

Following the snake's advice he went to Ayodhya. He presented himself at the palace under a different name and was soon employed as a charioteer. At night he would lie tossing on his bed, wondering what could have become of Damayanti. Had she reached her father's home? Was she angry with him? Was she unhappy as he was, because of their separation? Meanwhile Damayanti was also asking herself many questions. Where could Nala be? Why did he leave her? Would she ever see him again?

Damayanti was determined to find Nala. She spoke to her father about a plan. She composed a song which described the events in the forest. The last line of the song was a question, asking where the gambler had gone. Gathering many minstrels from the palace, she told each one to go from place to place, singing this song. If anyone should show interest in the song or attempt to sing a reply, the minstrel was to return and inform Damayanti.

The minstrels set out and travelled all over the continent singing Damayanti's song. They visited the villages, the inns, the bazaars, the towns and the palaces. Everywhere, where there was human habitation, a minstrel would go. For many months nothing happened. Damayanti was almost giving up hope of ever finding Nala again. Then one day, a minstrel returned and asked to see Damayanti. He told her that he had sung this song at the court of the king of Ayodhya. The king had praised the song and given him an extra gold piece because it delighted him so much. As the minstrel was leaving the palace, the king's charioteer came up to him. A wizened, ugly-looking man, he had been moved to tears on hearing the song. He asked the minstrel where he had come from. Then he replied to the minstrel's song with a song of his own, in which the gambler explains why he left his loved one.

Damayanti could hardly contain her joy. She was sure that the charioteer was Nala. Although the minstrel's description of the man did not fit that of Nala's, all the same, she began to think of ways and means of bringing him to her father's palace. Finally, she called a trusted friend of her father's and asked him to leave forthwith for Ayodhya and there inform the king that Damayanti, tired of waiting for Nala, was going to hold a second svayamvara very soon.

The message was conveyed. The king of Ayodhya sent for Nala. 'Tell me, my good friend,' he asked, 'can you drive me to the king of Vidarbha's palace within a day? I have just received a message from the king. His daughter Damayanti has waited many years for Nala who has not returned. Therefore she has declared her willingness to hold another svayamvara, and choose another husband. I must arrive there by tonight, as the ceremony is tomorrow morning.' Hearing these words, Nala's heart sank. 'How could she punish me in this manner?' he thought. 'I can't believe it. But it is my fault. I cannot blame her.' Aloud, he said to the king, 'As you wish, sir. You shall be there tonight.'

The horses raced as they had never raced before. But this was not just a mad scamper. The charioteer had complete control over them and the king marvelled at the skill with which he turned corners, side-stepped large stones and avoided the hanging branches of the trees. At times the king could have sworn that they had risen into the air, so swift was the pace of the chariot, and so smooth.

The king and his charioteer fell into conversation. At one point they found themselves in disagreement over the possible number of leaves and nuts on a certain tree which they had passed. The charioteer insisted that he was right. But the king kept saying that, being an expert at playing with dice, his knowledge about numbers was greater than that of the charioteer's. The charioteer insisted on stopping the chariot and began counting the leaves. The king was desperate, as they were losing time. The charioteer discovered that the king had been right, and humbly apologized to him. The king laughed and they began their journey again. Nala asked the king how he too could acquire the same skill. So the king generously said, 'If you tell me what lies behind your skill with horses, I shall tell you the secret of playing dice.' This was exactly what Nala had wanted and he listened eagerly as the king explained his secrets to him. At last Nala had acquired the knowledge that would enable him to win back his kingdom and fetch Damayanti from her parents' home. His mind became clear once more, for Kali had left him. But he again remembered in sorrow that it was probably too late. If Damayanti held her svayamvara the next morning, Nala would be unable to claim her. Sadly, he drove on.

On arriving at their destination, the king of Ayodhya was surprised to find no sign of preparations for the ceremony. Life was going on much as usual. Although he was received very warmly, the palace officers seemed surprised at his arrival and could not understand why he had driven post-haste from Ayodhya. Damayanti, of course, had not told anyone that she had had a message sent to him. Nala meanwhile had been conducted to another part of the palace, where he took the horses.

Damayanti, hearing that the king of Ayodhya had been driven by his expert charioteer, sent one of her attendants to talk to him. The maid at first enquired after Nala's welfare. Then she repeated the story that the minstrel had told and Nala confirmed the reply he had given. The maidservant rushed back to Damayanti with a report. Damayanti, for a final proof, sent the servant again, accompanied by the two children. Nala, on seeing them, recognized them as his own children and took them in his arms. When the maid questioned him, he said, 'I'm sorry. They remind me of my own children, and as I am away from them, I miss them.' The maid took the children back to Damayanti and told her what had happened.

Nala was summoned to the main palace. The servants told him that the princess wished to speak to him. He entered Damayanti's room. She was seated in the same corner where he had first seen her and she was wearing the same clothes she had on when he had left her in the forest. Although Nala was still in the ugly disguise, Damayanti recognized him. She asked him why he had left her and he explained that he had not known what he was doing. He was almost driven mad by the god of Darkness who was in him. But now the god of Darkness had left and Nala knew that he had been at fault. He asked for forgiveness but he added, 'It is too late now, for tomorrow you must choose another husband. Why did you not wait a little longer, my Damayanti?'

This time it was Damayanti's turn to explain. She replied, 'Forgive me for this pretence. I had never wished to marry anyone else. But I had to think of some way in which to bring you here after I had heard the minstrel's story. So I sent a friend with the message about the svayamvara. You will see that no other king has been invited. My mother alone knows my plans.' Nala was calm and happy. His fears were at an end. The god of Darkness had left him. He had acquired the skill he needed at dice. He remembered the two garments and the snake. Hastily he put them on and thought of his encounter with the snake. Immediately he was transformed into his original self.

There was much rejoicing at the palace. The king of Ayodhya complimented Damayanti on her brilliant plan and agreed to give Nala every help in regaining his kingdom. After a few days, Nala returned to Nishada and challenged his brother to a game of dice. He won back his throne and his kingdom. He returned to Vidarbha and fetched Damayanti and the two children. This time, they lived together happily to the end of their days.

The Four Young Men

A king once found himself in the company of a goblin with magical powers. 'I am going to ask you a riddle, king,' said the goblin, 'and if you cannot give me the right answer I shall strike you on your head and kill you.' And with these words the goblin proceeded to tell this story. . . . .

*

A man and his wife lived happily together in a large town. They had four sons whom they loved very much. The man took great care to educate them, according to the custom of the time. The boys were made to recite hymns; they had to learn the rules of grammar and multiplication tables; they spent many hours trying to write in neat letters. Then suddenly, the father and mother died and the boys were orphaned. They were bewildered and did not know what to do. The eldest suggested that since their grandfather was still alive, they should all go to the town where he and other relatives lived. So they went and their grandfather welcomed them with much affection. To begin with the four brothers lived happily with their relatives. They started learning grammar and mathematics again and recited hymns.

The eldest brother had brought whatever remained of their parents' money with him. With it the four of them paid for their tuition, their food and their clothes. There wasn't very much money, so they had to be careful and spend only a little at a time. Their cousins, who also lived in the same town, were rich. They began to make fun of the four brothers and tease them about their being poor.

One day the eldest brother could bear it no longer. Rather than be made fun of by the cousins, he thought he would kill himself. So he took a rope, went to the park and began tying it to the branch of a tree, with the intention of hanging himself. Just then a man passed by and seeing the rope, he stopped. 'What are you doing?' he asked. The young man shrugged his shoulders and explained, 'I am poor and my cousins keep on making fun of me and my three brothers. So I cannot stand it any longer. I have decided to hang myself.' The man was silent for a moment and then he said, 'You know, you mustn't lose heart so easily. If your cousins tease you, do not let it bother you.' 'But our poverty makes us helpless,' pleaded the young man. 'Why should you remain poor?' asked the man. 'You have been well educated by your parents. A good education and common sense are all you need to go out and seek a fortune. Now, why don't you take my advice? Don't hang yourself. Go back to your brothers and let each of you make himself a master of some type of knowledge or profession. In doing this you will be able to prove to the world that you are better than your cousins.' The young man thought deeply about what the stranger had said and then agreed that it would be better for him to go back to his brothers than to hang himself.

When he arrived home, he related his story to his brothers. They all agreed that it was a good idea that each of them should study a special subject. They also decided to separate for one year. Each one would go his own way in the pursuit of knowledge. At the end of the year, they would all meet again in the town at a particular place and exchange their views.

The year passed quickly. At the end of the twelve months, the four brothers met as arranged. They were naturally delighted to be with each other again. But soon, each began to brag about what he had learnt. The first brother stated, 'If I am given a bone, I can cast a spell so that it gets covered with flesh.' 'Why, that's nothing,' said the second. 'I can even produce the skin and the

31

hair on a piece of flesh.' 'Is that all?' remarked the third brother. 'I can turn the flesh and the bone into a limb—in fact, into the limb of the animal to which the bone belonged; and what's more, I can turn it into any number of limbs too.' 'Well,' said the fourth brother, 'it seems that I have made the best use of my time. I know the means of giving life to an object.' And thus they boasted, each of his newly acquired power.

One of them then suggested that they should go outside the town and test their knowledge. This idea was greeted with delight, since each of the brothers was burning to show off what he knew. So they went into the forest and began to look for a bone. They found one at last and the first brother was called upon to show what he could do. He spoke the magic words and soon the bone was covered with flesh. So the other three agreed that he had proved his knowledge. The second brother cast his spell and soon the flesh was covered with skin and hair and became a tawny colour. He too, had proved his skill. The third brother used what knowledge he had and the form took on the shape of a lion, since the bone had been that of a lion. The head appeared and then the four legs and the tail. There it lay on the ground, a large lion. The third brother too, had passed the test. It was now the turn of the fourth brother. He rubbed his hands gleefully and said, 'We were wise to have taken the advice of the stranger. We have all learnt our lessons well and shall soon prove our wisdom to the world.' Whereupon he too, spoke the magic words he had learnt and the lion sprang to life. Indeed, the four brothers had learnt their lessons well but alas, they used them foolishly. For the lion, as it came to life, was a large, hungry beast and it soon devoured all four brothers.

*

So ended the goblin's story. He turned to the king and said, 'Now, my question to you, king, is that of the four brothers, whose fault was it that they were all devoured by the lion?' The king thought for a while and then answered, 'It was the fault of the fourth brother. The first three did not know what sort of animal they were creating. But the fourth brother, seeing that it was a lion, should not have given it life. He was too eager to prove his knowledge. But he should have done so on some harmless creature.'

'Yes,' replied the goblin, 'but that was too easy a riddle. This time you are free to go, king. Next time, I shall ask you a more difficult one.'

And the goblin disappeared.

The Spell

There was once a man who lived in a town in northern India. He spent many years studying ancient books and talking to learned priests who came to visit the city. After much effort, he obtained the knowledge of a spell. He was very proud of this and guarded the secret carefully. When the moon and the stars were in a particular position in the sky and he repeated the spell in a certain way, seven precious stones would fall from the sky into his hands.

In order not to arouse people's suspicions as to where his money was coming from, he used to teach pupils from time to time. He had one pupil of whom he thought very highly. This young man knew about the spell but he did not know the secret of how it worked. One day, the teacher and his pupil left the town and began a journey to a neighbouring country. The first day of the journey went well and they slept the night in a small town near the frontier. But the next day, soon after they had set out, they found themselves in a deserted part of the country. The road ran through a dried-up river course and on each side of them rose cliffs, rugged rocky cliffs which seemed to cut them off from the sight and sound of any other human being. It was a hot day, the air was still and the sun, shining down on them, seemed to set them on fire. Nor were there any trees to provide some shade. So they perspired and trudged on.

They consoled themselves with the thought that they would soon be out of this deserted place. They began telling each other what they would do as soon as they arrived at the next village. Would they make for the village well or just collapse in the shade of a friendly house? Suddenly, they heard much shouting and scrambling and, on looking up, saw that the place was swarming with bandits. Some were down the road and others emerged in front of them. Their faces were partly covered with the ends of the turbans which they had wound round their heads and each one was brandishing a sword or a fearsome knife in his hand. There was no escape for the teacher and his pupil, as they were surrounded.

The unfortunate two were soon tied with ropes and carried to the bandits' hide-out, which was not far from the road. Both men were terrified, since they did not have much money on them. The bandits, they thought, would naturally be very annoyed when they discovered that the two prisoners were almost penniless. And so they were. But they had a method of dealing with such a situation. 'We shall demand a ransom for you before we set you free,' declared their chief. 'The older man can remain here with us but the younger one must return to his home town and collect the money.' 'Don't be anxious,' said the pupil to the teacher, reassuringly. 'I shall definitely be back with the money in a few days. May I beg you though, not to try out your spell in an effort to pay the ransom because if the bandits discover that you have the power to produce precious stones, they will never set you free.' With these words, the pupil departed.

That evening when it became dark, the teacher was lying on the ground outside the hide-out. He was still chained and his hands were tied. Looking up at the sky, he noticed with excitement that the moon and stars were in the right position for him to recite his spell. He argued with himself for a while about the advice that his pupil had given him. In the end he thought he would be better off if he paid for the ransom with the jewels that would fall from the sky and decided to recite his spell. So he called the bandit chief and said, 'You have sent my pupil to fetch a ransom for me but I wonder if he will return. If I were to give you quantities of jewels instead by this evening, would that satisfy you?' 'Indeed it would,' replied the chief. 'But how will you do that?' 'Please order your guards to cut the ropes and remove the chains that bind me,' said the old man. This was promptly done, though the guards remained suspicious.

The old man withdrew to a little distance and after a short while, he recited the spell. Within a matter of moments there fell into his hands, seven large and precious gems. He returned with these to the bandit chief, who, seeing them, was overjoyed. The prisoner was released immediately, was permitted to bathe and was invited to eat with the bandit chief that night. There was much rejoicing among the bandits. They had never in their profession come upon so much wealth from one man alone. Whilst the old man was eating his fill with the chief, the other bandits began to murmur, 'We should not let him go. He may come in useful again. He is a walking treasure-house.'

After the merry-making of the night, the bandits broke camp and decided to move to another part of the country. They invited the teacher to go with them. He accepted this invitation as he was afraid to break away from them so soon and thought it would be wiser if he remained with them until they came to the next village. So the entire troop moved off. But they had not gone very far when another group of five hundred bandits swooped down on them and began to rob them.

The chief bandit of the first troop turned to the leader of the second group and said, 'Why are you robbing us? We are merely bandits like yourselves and haven't great riches on us. If you really want treasure, then capture that old man there. He can make jewels fall out of the sky.' The poor teacher had hardly had time to understand what was going on when the second group of robbers fell upon him and made him captive. They demanded the same amount of treasure as he had given to the earlier bandits. He pleaded that he was willing to give it to them, but only in a year's time. 'Why must we wait for a year?' asked the chief. 'Because I can only recite my spell when the moon and the stars are in a certain position,' replied the teacher, 'and it will take a full twelve months before that happens again. Last night I managed to obtain the gems because the moon and the stars were in the correct position.' 'Wretch,' shouted the chief bandit. 'You lie in order to save your life. Off with his head,' he ordered his followers. The man was soon cut to pieces.

The conflict between the two bands of robbers now became heated. The second band realized that the first band must have the gems given to them by the dead man hidden in their clothes. So the two groups fought each other with their swords and knives until eventually, all but two of the bandits were killed. These two went round and collected all the treasure in one heap and then hid it in some nearby bushes.

It was noon by now and they were both very hungry. So they decided that one of them should stay near the treasure and guard it, while the other one would go to the village in the neighbourhood and buy some food. So one of them placed his sword near the treasure and kept guard over it and the other bandit set off in the direction of the village. Now, the one who sat and guarded the treasure thought, 'It is a pity that this treasure has to be divided into two. It would be so much simpler if I could take it all. We have already killed so many people, that it will not matter if I kill the other bandit as well. So I will wait here in readiness. As soon as he approaches with the food, I will spring on him and cut him down with my sword.' And so he waited in readiness to kill the other bandit.

Meanwhile, the other bandit had had similar thoughts. 'Why should I have to share the treasure with this man, after the trouble we have had in collecting it?' he said to himself. 'It is very simple. I will eat my fill in the village. Then I will buy some food for the other bandit and put poison into it so that when he eats it he will die.' And he did accordingly. He ate his fill in the village, bought some more food for the bandit who was waiting for him and mixed some poison with it. Then he returned to where the treasure was being guarded.

As he approached the bushes where the treasure had been hidden, he called out to the other bandit to come and eat. The bandit emerged from behind the bushes, took the food from him and almost immediately struck him with his sword and killed him. He hastily pushed the corpse out of the way and, being very hungry, sat down to eat. The food being poisoned, soon he too was dead. The treasure thus lay unguarded in the bushes.

The next day, the pupil having collected the ransom money, returned along the same road, looking for the first band of robbers, in order to pay the ransom and free his teacher. He followed the road until he saw all the bandits lying there, dead. He saw the body of his teacher and thought, 'Alas, he must have boasted about his power and shown them what he could do.' Then he counted all the corpses. There were nine hundred and ninety-eight bodies. He realised that there must have been a fight over the treasure. 'But two have got away,' he thought. He looked round and searched in the bushes. There they were, the last two, and not far away was the heap of jewels.

He shook his head sadly. 'So much killing, over a handful of jewels. If only my teacher had taken my advice and not tried to produce the treasure.'

Worldly Wisdom

There was once a king who had three sons. He should have been happy with his sons but he was not, because the boys were interested only in idling away their time. They refused to learn anything useful. The king invited the best teachers and the most learned men in the land to try and teach them sense and give them an education. But the boys continued to be lazy and idle. The king began to despair. How could he permit them to govern the kingdom after his death if they remained so stupid? While he was fretting about the future of his sons, the king was told of a particularly clever brahman who might be willing to try to educate them.

The brahman was sent for. He was an old man of eighty and he listened carefully to the tale of woe related by the king. When the king had finished speaking, he remained silent for a few minutes. The king could not understand the man's silence. He had promised him untold wealth and any luxury the man might want, provided he could make intelligent young men of his idle sons. Finally, the brahman replied, 'I do not want your wealth. You may reward me in whatever way you think fit after you have seen what I make of your sons. For the moment, give me leave to take them away with me for six months. At the end of six months, I shall bring them back to you and then you can test them.' The king was very surprised. The other brahmans whom he had spoken to had all demanded large sums of money as fees. The king was also suspicious, since he thought that this man would not be able to do much in six months. All the same, he gave him permission to take his sons away from the court for six months.

The next morning the three boys set out with their teacher. They walked in a casual manner and treated the new venture as another type of amusement. The brahman took them to his hermitage. This was a simple hut of leaves and thatch at the edge of the forest. For six months, he told them stories. These stories were about men and women and about animals. He explained each story to them and made them remember it. At the end of six months, he took the boys back to the king. All the courtiers were assembled and received them with due respect. Then they started questioning the boys as to what they thought about various matters dealing with good and bad conduct, making friends and enemies, how a king should rule and so on. To their great surprise, instead of giving the usual silly answers, the three princes were now replying with great wisdom and intelligence.

The king was amazed and demanded the secret from the brahman. But he merely said that he had told them stories which were full of wisdom, and, because they understood the stories, they saw the wisdom in them. Among the many stories which he told were the following:

THE BLUE JACKAL

There was once a jackal who lived in a forest at the edge of a town. Although he spent many hours wandering through the forest searching for food, he always had great difficulty in catching small animals. So one day he decided to go into the town and see if he would fare better, searching for scraps. That night he wandered stealthily through the streets.

He happened to pass a house where a dog had been tied in the courtyard. The dog, seeing the strange jackal, began to bark very loudly. Hearing the dog bark, all the other dogs in the neighbourhood took up the theme and there was a terrible noise. The poor jackal, terrified out of his wits, raced away down a narrow street. At the end of the street was the house of a dyer who had left a large vat of blue dye by his door at the edge of the street. The jackal, as he raced down the street, kept turning round to see if the dogs were following him, and thus, not being able to see the vat in time, fell straight into it.

Having lost trace of the jackal, the dogs gave up the chase. The jackal managed to pull himself out of the vat and slunk back into the forest. He discovered that his body was now of a rich blue colour. He was sitting downcast under a tree not knowing what to do and wondering how to get rid of the colour when he overheard some other animals talking. 'What a strange creature this is,' said one of them. 'How noble he looks in his rich hue. I wonder if he is some special royal animal which we have not seen before.' These remarks gave the jackal an idea. He got up, stretched himself in a leisurely manner and walked over to where the animals were talking. On seeing him approach, the animals rushed away in terror. But he called out to them gently and announced, 'Do not be afraid, animals of the forest. I am your new king, specially sent to rule over you. As long as you obey me, I shall do you no harm.'

On hearing this, the animals took courage and came back. They accepted him as king and obeyed all his commands. Even the tigers and the lions believed him to be a royal animal. So the jackal held court in the forest. The animals hunted and brought him food and he was always given the best meat of whatever was killed. He took good care, of course, not to have any jackals around him. This pleased the other animals, because the jackal is a sly animal and therefore not very popular with the other inhabitants of the forest.

Weeks and months went by and the blue jackal reigned supreme. But after some time he began to feel lonely. There was nobody for him to talk to. He had no friends as he had sent all the jackals away. One day, whilst he was sitting in full court and giving orders to a lion, he heard a pair of jackals calling out in the forest. He was so excited by the call of one of his own kind that without thinking, he answered back with a piercing howl. In a flash, the lions realized that the blue jackal was no royal animal. He was merely a jackal. They were furious at having been fooled and immediately fell upon him and tore him to pieces.

Thus, those who leave their friends and pretend to be what they are not, come to an unhappy end.

THE MICE THAT SET THE ELEPHANTS FREE

A large clan of mice lived happily in the ruins of an old temple. The little mice would bask in the sun for hours on end, quite undisturbed, since no one passed that way. But one day, a calamity befell the clan. A herd of elephants came walking through the forest, past the ruins, in search of water. The coming of the elephants was so unexpected that the mice, especially the little ones, had no time to scamper away. A number of them were crushed beneath the heavy elephants. When the elephants had passed, the mice gathered together and there was much lamenting and wailing over the dead ones.

One of the mice then declared, 'Brothers, this has been a truly terrible day. We cannot permit this to happen again. If the elephants decide to pass this way again, there will be nothing left of our clan. Therefore we must take counsel. Either we move to another place or else we ask the elephants to take another route.' This proposal was greeted with enthusiasm and hastily, the elders of the community went into a special hole where the meetings were held and decisions were taken. Although all the elders agreed that it would be better to ask the elephants to take another route, the problem was, how were the elephants to be approached? And, besides, who was to be sent to make this request? Every mouse present was afraid that the elephants would be angry at such a request and would merely trample on the messenger.

Finally, it was decided to send a mission. A number of mice from amongst the elders were selected. The mission went to the lake where the elephants were bathing, walked up to where the chief of the elephants sat and bowed low to the ground in great respect. The elephant acknowledged their bow and asked them what they wanted. In trembling voices, the mice explained why they had come and requested the elephants to be so gracious as to take another route on their way to the lake. The elephant thought for a while and then replied, 'Your request seems very reasonable to me. It does not make much difference to us whether we pass by the temple or at a little distance away from it. Therefore, return to your community and tell them that we shall not disturb you in future.' The mice were delighted with the news and returned to their old occupations without the constant fear of the coming of the elephants.

Now it so happened that one day, whilst the elephant herd, including their chief, was wandering through the forest, they fell into a trap. The trap had been laid by some elephant-catchers who were very pleased at having succeeded. They tied the elephants with ropes to the trees and thus imprisoned them. Since it was getting dark the elephant-catchers decided to leave the elephants there for the night. Having made sure that the elephants were securely tied, they went away.

The elephants were naturally very frightened at having been caught. Since they were tied with ropes, there was little they could do to escape. 'Is there nobody who could set us free?' they wondered. The chief of the elephants thought for a while. He thought of all the mighty beasts of the forest, the lions, the tigers, the leopards, the wild buffaloes, who were all close friends of his but he knew that none of them would be of any help. Suddenly he remembered the mice. 'I made a pact of friendship with them,' he thought. 'I treated it as a joke at the time, but it might come in useful now. They would be able to help us out and perhaps free us by gnawing at the ropes.' So he summoned

a bird who was his friend and asked him to fly to the clan of mice in the ruins of the temple and explain to them what had happened.

The elephants were so nervous at having been trapped and so tired with trying to escape, that towards midnight they were beginning to doze off from sheer exhaustion. All at once they heard a scampering, slithering sound. What could it be? And then from behind a tree, emerged the vast clan of mice. There were many families of grandparents, parents, sons, daughters, grandchildren, cousins, uncles and aunts and many distant relatives. They exchanged a rapid greeting with the elephants and then the elders began to survey the situation. In a matter of moments they had decided what was to be done and orders were given accordingly. Then began the greatest gnawing and chewing that the mouse clan had ever been called upon to do. They gnawed and they chewed away until the early hours of the morning. As the sun rose and darted through the branches of the trees, the last of the ropes was chewed apart and the elephant herd was free. When the elephant-catchers arrived later in the morning, great was their astonishment to see nothing but a mass of chewed rope and no elephants at all.

Thus, it is always wise to have friends—many friends—and it does not matter whether they are strong or weak.

THE CAVE THAT TALKED

There was once a lion who had hunted all day in the forest but had caught nothing. He walked on, feeling desperately hungry and very tired. It was getting dark and he knew that there would be few animals around at that time, as most return home by dusk. Suddenly he saw a cave in a hill nearby. 'This is a bit of luck,' he thought. 'I shall go into the cave and hide myself. Some animal is sure to come there to sleep at night. I can then eat a good dinner without making an effort to catch it first.' So he went into the cave and waited.

The cave was the home of a jackal. He slept there every night. As it grew dark, the jackal returned from his day's activities to the cave. '*Hello-o-o-*,' he called. There was silence. 'Strange,' said the jackal loudly. 'What's the matter with you, Cave? You always reply to my greeting. If you're going to be unfriendly tonight, I shall go to another cave.'

The lion, hearing this, thought, 'The poor cave must be terrified because I am here. Perhaps that is why he does not greet the jackal in the usual manner. I think I shall reply instead.' So he shouted back, '*Hello-o-o.*' And the roar of the lion resounded through the cave and through the forest. The jackal chuckled to himself as he hastily ran off in another direction, priding himself on his cleverness. The roar had also warned the animals that the lion was inside the cave, so they kept away. Thus the poor lion had no meal that night.

In an uncertain situation it is better to be cautious and test the surroundings than to rush in and suffer regret. Even the majestic lion can fall into the trap of the shrewd jackal.

THE MONGOOSE WHOSE LOYALTY WAS DOUBTED

A man and his wife lived with their small son and a pet mongoose. The wife was very fond of the mongoose and brought it up almost as if it were a child. But all the same, she remained a little suspicious of it and was always frightened that it might harm her son.

One day she set out to collect water from the village well, which was rather far away. She put her son into his cradle and told her husband to keep an eye on him and the mongoose. Soon after she had left, her husband, being extremely greedy, decided that he would go out and quickly get some food and return before his wife got back. As he was a priest, he could easily ask for alms. So he left the mongoose in the same room as the child and set out.

A little while later, the mongoose noticed a large, black snake wriggling across the floor of the room. The snake was going in the direction of the cradle. The mongoose was ready for a fight, both because the snake is its natural enemy and because it thought that the snake would harm the child. It waited for the right moment. Then it sprang on the snake, caught it by its neck and shook it hard. When the snake was quite dizzy, he knocked its head on the ground. To make sure that the snake was dead, the mongoose tore it to bits. Then, feeling happy at having saved the child's life, he rushed out to meet the wife, whom he heard coming.

But the wife, seeing the blood on the mongoose, immediately thought that the animal had killed her child. In fury, she struck the mongoose with her pitcher with such force that the animal died on the spot. Then she rushed home and found that her child was gurgling in his cradle, while the scattered remains of the dead snake lay on the floor. She realised what had in fact happened—that the mongoose had saved the life of her child. She was now full of sorrow at what she had done.

Thus, it is better not to act in haste than to regret the action afterwards.

Sassi and Punnu

Across the desert of Thar in western India, camel caravans travel in many directions. These are long lines of camels carrying saddle-bags full of merchandise, walking with a rolling gait, with the caravan leader sitting on the foremost camel. The many hours of travelling through the desert can be monotonous. To while away the time, the people travelling as part of the camel caravan, sing songs. They sing about the places they have visited and the stories they have heard. There is one song which is particularly popular. It is a sad song. The story concerns the two lovers, Sassi and Punnu. . . . .

*

A man and his wife lived in a city called Bhambhor on the banks of the mighty River Indus. They had every happiness in the world except one: they had no children. Day and night they prayed at the temple, asking the gods to grant them a child. For years no child was born to them. But after many years, the wife gave birth to a girl. They were full of joy at having a child at last. A lavish celebration was held at which half the town was invited to feast and make merry. In accordance with their family custom, the man had a horoscope made for the child by the local priest.

But the horoscope held bad news. 'Your daughter will be intelligent, lively and lovely to look at,' said the priest. 'She will be all you could wish for in a child. But she will marry a man of another religion.' The superstitious parents having had a horoscope made and read, now, foolishly, felt that this was as bad as

49

a death sentence. How could they ever survive the disgrace of their daughter marrying into another religion? The man and his wife were very disappointed and they cursed the day that the child had been born. After much thought, they decided that they would get rid of the baby. So they put the child into a small wooden box and floated the box on the river.

The box bumped against the banks as it was carried along by the current. A few miles downstream was the place where the washermen did their washing. One of them was standing knee-deep in water, soaking some clothes, when he saw the box. He waded across to it and caught it. There was naturally much interest in its contents. Imagine the washermen's surprise when they found in the box, a small baby girl.

Delighted, each one played with the child in turn. They rushed back to the part of the town where they lived and called their wives to see the child. What were they to do with it? The washerman who had found the box, asked the others if he and his wife could keep the baby and bring her up as their own child, since they had no children. This was readily agreed to. After all, it was fair enough, since he was the first to have spotted the box. They named the child Sassi, which means "the moon", since her bright face, wreathed in smiles, reminded them of the moon.

Sassi was happy in her new home. Her foster parents fussed over her as they would have over their own child. As she grew older, all the neighbours began to remark on her qualities and her intelligence. Sassi had such gentle ways that some people were jealous. She was clearly the joy of the community of washermen and their families. She used to run errands for her father and deliver the clothes when they had been washed. Many people in Bhambhor knew her and praised her qualities.

A number of caravan routes crossed at the town of Bhambhor. It thus became a centre where people from the neighbouring countries met, in exchanging their wares. The description and fame of Sassi spread from Bhambhor to places far away. The

traders would return to their homes and talk about Sassi. Across the desert was a country ruled by a king who had four sons. The youngest of the four was called Punnu. He used to spend many hours wandering through the market-place and sitting in the caravanserais, where the merchants would meet and gossip and tell each other tales about the fabulous countries which they had visited.

Punnu was sitting in one of these inns one evening when the conversation turned to Bhambhor. Some merchants had just returned from there. 'Did you see any marvels there?' asked Punnu. 'Yes, I saw the greatest marvel of them all,' one merchant replied. 'I saw the living moon.' 'What are you referring to?' asked Punnu. 'I saw Sassi,' was the reply. 'Why is she the living moon?' said Punnu, who was now becoming interested in this marvel. 'If the moon should choose to come down and live among mortals, she could choose no better form than that of Sassi,' laughed the merchant. 'But Sassi, our Sassi of Bhambhor, is the simple daughter of a washerman. In fact, she isn't even that. No one knows whose daughter she is. Perhaps she is the moon in human form after all.'

Punnu was most intrigued by these remarks. Was she really as remarkable as everyone described her, he wondered? If so, she should be worth seeing. He thought of how he could contrive to see Sassi without attracting attention. Being a prince, it would soon be talked about if he showed an interest in meeting the daughter of a washerman. So he dressed as a merchant and collecting some goods and a few camels, he set out. He told his father that he was going to see the world for a few months and in order to see it better would travel disguised as a merchant. The king was delighted with the adventurous spirit of his son and wished him luck.

On arriving at Bhambhor, the prince settled down in an inn. The news soon spread in the city that a young merchant had arrived and was selling some rare things—perfumes, beads, and embroidered cloths—such as had not been seen before. People flocked to the inn to see and buy his wares. Sassi also heard of the merchant and, being very fond of beads, wanted to see what he had for sale. She asked her father if she could go there with her friend, Rakhi, and he agreed.

The two friends set out. They came to the inn where the young merchant had his stall. Sassi was fascinated by the beads. Never had she seen such a collection of differently shaped beads in such a range of colours. She was curious about where they came from. When she had chosen the ones she wanted, she held them in her hand and turned to the merchant to ask him the price. But she found the merchant staring at her, not having heard a word of what she had said. And as she looked at him, she slowly stopped speaking and the beads were left in her outstretched hand.

The merchant recovered with a start and rapidly counted the beads and asked for a small price, far less than the beads were worth. He wondered who this lively and beautiful young woman was. As the two friends walked out of the inn, Punnu asked in a casual voice, 'Who were those two gentle girls?' 'Good heavens, man,' replied the innkeeper, 'have you never heard of the famed Sassi of Bhambhor? The younger of the two was Sassi.' 'The one who bought the beads?' asked Punnu, who could hardly control his excitement. 'That's right,' replied the innkeeper. 'I'm sure you have no one who could equal her in the part of the world that you come from.' Punnu had to admit that Sassi indeed deserved her fame.

Meanwhile, Rakhi noticed that Sassi had become very quiet. Her thoughts seemed far away. When she asked jokingly if she had any young man on her mind, Sassi blushed and changed the conversation. One day Sassi had to admit to Rakhi that she had lost her heart to the young merchant. She begged Rakhi to help her find out if he loved her too. Punnu, still in the guise of a merchant, was pining for Sassi all this while. He could think of nothing but her. Wherever he went he kept hoping that he would see Sassi again. At last he could bear it no longer so he decided that he would speak to her friend, Rakhi.

Soon after Sassi had begged Rakhi to help her, Punnu met Rakhi in the street and admitted to her that he was in love with Sassi and would not rest until he had married her. Rakhi was of course delighted that the young merchant felt the same way about Sassi as Sassi felt about him. She agreed to enquire of Sassi's father as to whether he was willing to allow his daughter to marry the merchant. She comforted Punnu with the fact that Sassi had vowed she would marry no one but him. Punnu had also decided that he would marry none other than Sassi. Rushing back to Sassi, Rakhi told her all that had passed and Sassi was overjoyed. But now they faced the next problem. Would her father agree to their being married? Since Sassi was very fond of her foster-parents, she did not wish to displease them. Yet, her love for Punnu was so great that she dreaded what would happen if they refused to give their consent.

That evening, Rakhi called on Sassi's parents. They were always glad to see her. She was not only their daughter's friend but, being the older of the two, they felt that she also looked after Sassi. In the course of the evening Rakhi said jokingly, 'Sassi is now old enough to be married. Have you found a husband for her yet?' Her father sighed and said thoughtfully, 'I don't know what to do. She must marry into my own community but among the young washermen I can't see anyone who is good enough for her.' 'And if such a washerman was to turn up, would you give your consent to a marriage?' asked Rakhi. 'I would be happy to do so,' was the reply.

The next day, Rakhi rushed off to the inn and spoke to Punnu. 'You can only marry Sassi if you pretend that you are a washerman,' she told him. 'Alas, but I have never even washed a handkerchief in my life,' said the mournful Punnu. 'Never mind. Leave that to me,' Rakhi said, encouragingly. So Punnu packed all his bags, loaded the camels, and told the innkeeper that he and his servants were moving on to the next city. Outside Bhambhor, Punnu ordered his servants to take the caravan back to his father's kingdom with the message that he would return in a few months' time and that his father was not to worry about him. When the caravan had departed, Punnu changed into the simple clothes worn by washermen and returned to Bhambhor.

The following day, Rakhi took him to Sassi's house. She told Punnu to wait in the courtyard while she went into the house herself. There she met Sassi's father and said to him, 'I have brought you a young washerman who wants to marry Sassi. Do go out and talk to him.' Sassi's father saw Punnu standing in the courtyard and commented, 'If the man is anything like his outward appearance, he will indeed make a good match for my Sassi. But appearances cannot be trusted. He must be a man who can work well.' He gave him a bundle of clothes which had just arrived and said, 'I wish to see how good you are at your trade, young man. Take these dirty clothes and wash and starch them. If I am satisfied with your work, I shall give my consent to your marrying Sassi.' So Punnu took the bundle of clothes and walked to the river bank. He opened the bundle and seeing a variety of clothes, felt completely lost. How should he begin and what should he do first?

Sassi, who had sat at a window when Punnu arrived, had heard the conversation. As soon as Punnu left, she beckoned to Rakhi. 'Rakhi, my dear friend, we must help him,' she said, 'else he will never be able to wash the clothes. You have already done so much for me and I am so grateful to you. Please make my happiness complete and help me now.' Rakhi put her arm round Sassi and smiled. 'Silly girl' she said affectionately, 'do you think I would stop helping you now when you need my help most? I am going down to the river bank in a few minutes and I will wash the clothes for Punnu. But listen, what worries me, is how am I going to starch them?'

'Oh leave that to me,' said Sassi joyfully. 'If you can somehow smuggle the clothes which need starching here, then tonight, when my parents are asleep, I will starch them.' So it was agreed. Rakhi helped Punnu wash the clothes and at night, Sassi starched them. By the early hours of the morning, Rakhi returned the bundle of starched clothes to Punnu.

At noon the next day, Punnu arrived at Sassi's house, carrying a large bundle of clothes on his head. He was received in the courtyard. 'I have brought the clothes, sir,' said Punnu to her father. 'What, have you washed them already? They couldn't have been done very well,' replied the washerman with suspicion. So Punnu opened the bundle and Sassi's father examined the clothes. 'But this is wonderful, young man,' he said. 'You are not only a fast worker, but your work is extremely good. With a husband like you, Sassi is bound to be happy and well cared for.' He gave his consent to the marriage. In a few weeks, Sassi and Punnu were married. They settled in Bhambhor and were very happy together.

Many months passed. Punnu's father waited eagerly for the return of his youngest son but there was no news of him. The king became anxious and sent his officers out to search for Punnu. After a long time they returned and reported that they had found Punnu in Bhambhor, where he had married the daughter of a washerman, and it seemed that he had no intention of returning to his own country. The king was very upset at this. He kept complaining that he should not have allowed Punnu to go in the first place. Seeing their father in this sorrowful state, Punnu's three elder brothers said to him, 'Please be comforted, dear father. If you permit us, we shall go to Bhambhor and bring Punnu back. I'm sure we shall be able to persuade him to return.'

The three brothers travelled across the desert and, on arriving at Bhambhor, went to Punnu's house. Punnu was naturally most happy to see his brothers again. They embraced each other with great affection. Punnu introduced them to Sassi and they remarked on the beauty of their sister-in-law. Sassi cooked them a sumptuous meal, with delicacies they had never tasted in the royal kitchen. They talked for hour after hour about Punnu's family and their home. Sassi began to feel sleepy, so she bade them good night and retired.

Some time later, one of the brothers suggested that they should celebrate their reunion. Punnu readily agreed. Thereupon, another brother unpacked a bottle of wine from his bag and they drank to each other's health. Suddenly Punnu began to feel very sleepy. He just couldn't keep his eyes open and fell back unconscious on the the cushions. Unseen by Punnu, the brothers had mixed a powder in his wine whereby he would remain unconscious for many hours. They hastily wrapped a large cloak round him, took him out to the courtyard where their camels were tethered, hoisted him on to a camel and tied him securely to it. Stealthily, the three brothers, with the unconscious Punnu, crept out of Bhambhor.

Sassi had been asleep. When she woke in the morning, she called out to Punnu but there was no reply. This puzzled her and she went from room to room, calling to him. But there was no sign of Punnu, and no sign either, of any of his brothers. She looked into the courtyard but the camels were gone. She ran down to the river bank where the washermen washed their clothes but no one had seen Punnu. Slowly she realised what had happened and why Punnu's brothers had come. They had kidnapped him and taken him back to his home. Sassi wept bitter tears but all the same was determined to follow them to their country and bring Punnu back.

So she wandered out of Bhambhor and started walking through the desert in the direction of Punnu's home. Sassi walked for hours. The sun rose high in the sky and the desert was scorching hot. There wasn't a single bush or a tree anywhere under which she could rest. On and on she went as if in a nightmare. Towards evening, it became a little cooler, but by now Sassi could hardly walk. She was dragging her feet, slowly and painfully. She saw a hut not far away and as she approached it, a man appeared. 'Please, sir,' she asked, 'have you seen my Punnu? He was with his three brothers and they were riding camels. Have they passed this way?' 'No', said the man. 'I haven't seen anyone pass this way. But you look ill and and tired. Would you care to rest in my hut?' 'No, thank you,' replied Sassi. 'I must go on and find my Punnu.' She started walking again painfully through the desert. The man became curious to know who this girl wandering through the desert alone was and he began following her. Seeing this, Sassi was terrified. She broke into a run. But her body was already far too exhausted and she collapsed on the desert sand. She was dead.

When Punnu awoke after many hours, he felt himself lurching in a most uncomfortable manner. He opened his eyes and the glare of the sun almost made him close them again. 'Where on earth am I?' he thought. Then he saw his brothers and the desert around him and felt his arms and legs tied to the camel. 'What's the meaning of all this?' he enquired. 'Am I dreaming?' 'No Punnu,' replied his eldest brother. 'You're on your way back home.' He explained to Punnu what they had done. Punnu was wild with anger. He cursed his brothers and demanded that he be allowed to return to Sassi. But the brothers merely smiled. Punnu realised that he would have to play a trick on them.

After a short while, he said he was thirsty. His brothers gave him some water. He started the conversation again and brought it round to Sassi. 'In fact, this is all for the best,' he told his brothers. 'I was getting rather tired of Sassi. It's pleasant to be a poor young man for a short while. It's great fun. But after all, I am a prince, and the life of a prince is far more pleasant.' The brothers were thrilled to hear this. They thought that they had won Punnu round to their way of thinking. Later, when Punnu said that the rope with which he was tied was hurting him, they decided to undo the knots altogether and allow him to ride freely on the camel. No sooner had they done this, than Punnu turned the camel round and raced back in the direction from which they had come. The brothers shouted to him to return and tried to catch him again but he was too fast for them.

Punnu raced the camel until it fell exhausted under him. So he left the camel and began walking. By nightfall he too was almost unconscious with fatigue. He fell asleep for a couple of hours and then awoke and started walking again. He continued thus for another day and another night, quenching his thirst with the muddy water of drying streams. On the third morning, he struggled up and clambered over a sand dune. In the distance he saw a hut. To one side of the hut was a dip between two sand dunes. Here a man was seated on the sand, staring at a small mound nearby.

The man looked up as Punnu staggered towards him. 'Who are you?' he asked. 'I am Punnu. Have you seen my Sassi anywhere? Has she passed this way?' Punnu enquired in a weak voice. The man nodded slowly. He got up and helped Punnu to walk across the mound. 'Yes, my friend,' he replied. 'She is now buried under this mound.' The man told him what had happened. He tried to comfort Punnu but Punnu sat there looking at the mound without saying a word. The man brought him water and some bread. But Punnu did not touch it. Suddenly he cried out aloud and cursed his fate, that his love for Sassi should have ended thus. He threw himself over the grave of Sassi. Punnu was dead.

The Barber's Wife

There was once a barber who was known as Clumsy-Fingers. Try as he might, the poor man could never cut a man's hair without cutting off a bit of his ear as well or shave a man without leaving gashes on his face. Naturally, people stopped coming to him and the barber became extremely poor. The less he earned the more his wife and children suffered. His wife was irritated at having to put up with a stupid husband.

One day, Clumsy-Fingers did not earn any money at all. He waited all day for customers but no one came. At the end of the day he had to face his wife with the fact that there was no money in the house. She said angrily to her husband, 'Why can't you earn at least enough to feed us each day even if you can't provide for any comforts? The pots have been scraped clean in the kitchen and there is nothing for us to eat tonight. I was hoping to buy some food with your earnings and now you tell me that you have made nothing all day.' Then, as she stamped out of the room, she shouted, 'If you can't earn any money, then go and beg for some.'

The barber thought this was a good idea. But where was he to go in order to beg for money? He asked his wife where he should go. She thought for a moment and then said, 'Why, the king is getting married today. Go to the palace and ask him for something.' Clumsy-Fingers nodded and set off.

On reaching the palace, he told the officers that he had a special request to make of the king. Ushered into the king's presence, he bowed respectfully and begged him to give him something. The king was amused and asked him what exactly he wanted. Clumsy-Fingers suddenly realized that he hadn't asked his wife what he should beg for, so he repeated, 'Just something, your Majesty.' The king laughed and ordered his minister to grant the barber some wasteland outside the city. The barber returned home delighted. 'Well,' asked his wife, 'what did the king give you?' 'Some land outside the city,' replied Clumsy-Fingers with a smile. 'Oh you foolish man,' said his wife. 'Since when have you become a farmer, asking for a piece of land? What are we going to do with it?'

When her anger had cooled a little, the barber's wife called out to Clumsy-Fingers and they both went to see the land. It was a large patch of uneven ground. The poor woman shrank with horror at the thought of the amount of work they would have to put into ploughing the land before they could plant anything on it. But she was never without an idea for long. She ordered her husband to imitate her movements and soon they were both walking slowly over the land, treading carefully, with their eyes on the ground, as if looking for something.

Whilst they were busy doing this, a band of robbers happened to pass that way. They were curious to know what the barber and his wife were looking for. The leader of the band approached the wife and asked her if they had lost something. She pretended to be startled by the man and quickly said, 'Oh no, no, no. Nothing at all. Nothing at all.' This made the robber even more suspicious and he tried to find out by phrasing his questions in various ways. But she was equally sharp-witted. After much questioning, she took the robber aside, made him swear that he would not tell anyone else what she was going to tell him and said, 'My uncle died a week ago. Before he died, he told me that he had buried five pots of gold in this field. We are trying to see if we can find them. But please don't tell a soul, else we shall lose our gold. The robber swore that he wouldn't tell anyone and left. Soon the barber and his wife returned home, the wife in high spirits.

The barber could not understand why his wife was suddenly

so pleased with the land. The next morning, they went back to look at the field. To their pleasant surprise, every inch of it had been dug. The barber's wife chuckled with glee as she explained her trick to her husband. 'I knew he would rush back and tell his friends what he had heard. The poor things must have spent all night toiling away, digging up the field in order to find the pots of gold. Now all we have to do is buy some grains of wheat and plant them.'

She went to the corn-merchant and bought the grain on credit and planted it. The harvest was magnificent, for the land had been really well dug. The barber's wife sold the grain for a large sum and they started living in greater comfort. But the robbers were very sore about the way they had been cheated by the barber's wife. So they were waiting for an opportunity to take revenge.

One evening, as it was getting dark, the leader of the robbers slipped into the barber's house and hid himself. When the barber's wife was preparing to sleep, she saw his shadow and recognized him. She went into the kitchen, took a shallow bowl and filled it with garbage. At the top she put a layer of sweets. Then she whispered to her husband that as soon as she was in bed he must ask her in a loud voice where she had put the money. She returned to the other room and got into bed. A few minutes later, her husband came into the room and asked, 'Where have you put the money? I hope it is in a safe place.' The barber's wife replied, 'Don't worry about that. It is very safe. I have put it at the bottom of the dish which has the sweets. No one will ever find it.' After this, the barber and his wife retired for the night.

The robber smiled and waited until the two were asleep. Then he crept into the kitchen, saw the bowl of sweets and made off with it. He returned to his companions and said, 'The silly woman thought the money was very safe but she won't see it again.' But he had been fooled once more, because all that the robbers found in the bowl was kitchen garbage under a layer of sweets. They swore that they would harass the barber's wife until they had robbed her of all the money.

A few nights later, when the barber's wife was going to bed, she heard some whispering outside her window and she recognized the voice of the robbers. 'So they are here again,' she said to herself. 'Well, I'll show them.' She listened very carefully and heard them say that they would climb in by the window. She hastily grabbed the barber's razor and waited beside the window. Soon she heard a gentle scraping on the outer wall. A face peered in through the window. Quick as lightning, she struck the robber's nose with the razor and sliced it off clean. The head disappeared immediately. The other robbers felt that he must have hit himself on something sharp. After all, no one sits by a window all night waiting to slice off a robber's nose. So the second robber tried his luck. But he tumbled down double-quick, also without his nose. All of them met with the same fate and had to return home without their noses.

When the summer had set in and the days were hot and the nights were cool, it was more pleasant to sleep out of doors than in a room. So the barber and his wife put their beds in the backyard, where the cool night breeze brought on a deep sleep. One night, the barber's wife dreamt that she was riding in a palanquin. It was very pleasant indeed. But at one stage it became rather jerky and she happened to open her eyes. Horror of horrors! She wasn't riding in a palanquin at all. Instead, her bed was being carried by four robbers, with three following. 'What shall I do?' thought the woman. 'I really have been trapped by them this time. I wonder where they are taking me. I can't expect much mercy from them now.'

Just then she heard one of them say, 'I suggest we take a short rest soon. She is terribly heavy and my shoulder is beginning to hurt.' 'Yes', said another, 'I feel tired too. Let's put the bed down under that banyan tree and take a brief nap.' This was agreed to

by all of them. The barber's wife had to think very fast. This was her only chance of escape. They placed the bed under the tree, lay down and dozed off. Carefully catching hold of a branch, she climbed up the tree. Fortunately, the banyan tree has big leaves and many roots that come down from the branches, so she was able to slowly raise herself onto the branch and sit there quite comfortably. So that the robbers would not suspect anything, she had arranged the bedclothes on the bed in such a shape that it appeared as though a person was asleep.

She bundled herself up and crouched on the branch of the tree. She wrapped her face and arms in her white shawl and let the ends flap. Just as they began to show signs of stirring and waking up, she started howling in a ghost-like manner. In the darkness and quiet of the night, the sound was terrifying. The robbers awoke and saw a white figure sitting on the tree, flapping its wings and howling. They were certain that it was a ghost and that the tree was haunted. So all seven of them took to their heels. They did not even glance back, so frightened were they. The barber's wife could hardly control her laughter. When they were completely out of sight, she climbed down from the tree, picked up her bed and walked home. The seven robbers were never heard of in that neighbourhood again.

The Oilpresser and the Devils

In a small village near Tiruchirapalli there lived an oilpresser. He used to earn his living from buying bags of sesame seeds, crushing them in his oil-mill and selling the sesame oil. But life was difficult for him. Sesame seeds were very expensive and he could not buy a large quantity. Each day he became poorer and poorer. At last he decided that what he needed was a new mill which would crush the seeds with greater force and thus perhaps produce a larger quantity of oil. Now the best oil mills are made from the wood of the tamarind tree. Fortunately for the oilpresser, there was a large tamarind tree in his back garden. His wife begged him not to cut down this tree because she used the fruit of the tamarind in cooking various dishes. But the oilman insisted, since he could not afford to buy the wood from the market.

He woke up early the next morning, bathed, took some fresh flowers to the shrine in the village where he always worshipped and prayed to god that the new mill might bring him a large income. He had consulted the priest as to the most auspicious moment to start cutting down the tree. The priest, after thumbing through a number of palm leaf manuscripts, told him that this would be at seventeen minutes past nine in the morning. So at nine-fifteen, the oilpresser stood ready by the tamarind tree with an axe. As soon as his wife said that it was exactly seventeen minutes past nine, he struck the tree with a mighty blow. His wife, who couldn't bear to see the tree being cut, went indoors.

What the oilpresser did not know was that the tamarind tree was the home of a devil. So when he struck the first blow, the devil became most alarmed. The devil's family, for many generations, had lived in the tree and therefore the devil had a sentimental attachment to it. In addition, it was a large tree and made a comfortable home. Naturally, he did not wish to move out and go through all the trouble of finding a new tree. So, after the first blow, he rushed out of the tree and fell at the feet of the oilpresser. The latter was terrified to see this strange creature. But he pretended he was not in the least bit frightened. 'Who are you and what do you want?' he asked the devil. 'I am the devil who lives in this tree. I have lived here for twenty-five years. This is my ancestral home. I beg of you not to destroy it. I shall do anything for you if you promise to spare the tree.'

The oilpresser, seeing that he was in a stronger position, wished to make sure that the devil meant what he said. 'I know your type,' he replied. 'You are meek and humble when you are in trouble. But the moment I agree not to harm your dwelling, you will go back on your word.' But the devil swore that he would keep to the bargain if the oilpresser spared the tree. 'Very well, then,' said the oilpresser. 'Listen to me carefully. I shall not cut down the tree and you can continue to live here but on one condition. You must supply me with 100 bags of sesame seed before the end of each month. And don't try any tricks with me. The moment you fail to produce the 100 bags, I shall immediately cut down the tree.' The devil swore that he would do as asked.

The tree was left standing and at the end of every month the oilpresser's courtyard was filled with 100 bags of sesame seed. Gradually he built up his business. One mill could not cope with such a large quantity of seeds, so he set up some more mills. Day and night, the creaking of the mills could be heard as they crushed the seeds and the oil poured out. The oilpresser became very rich. He bought up all the other mills in the village and became the biggest oilman in the region.

The oilpresser used bullocks for working the oil mills. They were tied to a pole and walked round in a circle so that the

wheels of the mill would turn and crush the seeds. The bullocks had to be young and energetic, as it was tiring work. There was one amongst them who was particularly frisky but worked very well. The oilpresser, in affection, had called it New Devil. One day, New Devil fell ill and the oilpresser was very upset. So he called in the man who knew all about animal diseases. He examined New Devil and said that the animal could only be cured by being branded with a red-hot iron. The oilpresser ordered his servants to prepare the iron.

Meanwhile the devil in the tamarind tree had been sitting, deep in thought. A friend of his, another devil, came to see him and asked him what the matter was. The devil of the tamarind tree confessed that he was worried because he had promised to provide the oilpresser with 100 bags of sesame seed before the end of each month. 'There has been a drought in this part of the country. With no rain, the sesame crop has failed and I have had to travel long distances to get the seeds. Now I fear that even those sources have been exhausted and I may not be able to get the bags before the end of this month. If I can't, then he will cut down this tree and I shall have to find another home.' And the poor devil was almost in tears.

'Oh, nonsense, my friend,' said the visitor. 'You should not be afraid of a mere man. After all, you are a devil. But let me deal with this oilpresser. You take your family and go and live in my house for a few days. I will live here and shall soon have the oilpresser begging for mercy from me.' The devil was very dubious and reluctant to go, but his friend persuaded him. So, packing a few things, he and his wife and child left the tamarind tree and went to live in the friend's house.

It was soon after this that New Devil fell ill and it was suggested that the bullock be branded. 'Where shall we do the branding?' asked the oilpresser. The doctor looked round and replied, 'Perhaps under the tamarind tree. It will be cooler there.' So the branding iron was taken to a spot under the tamarind tree where the fire was stoked and the iron made glowing hot. The devil in the tree was a little puzzled by what was going on. 'Who are they going to brand with that terrifying iron rod?' he asked himself. When the iron was glowing to a bright scarlet, the oilpresser shouted to one of the servants, 'Bring New Devil here.'

The devil in the tree naturally thought that New Devil referred to him, since he was the new devil in the tamarind tree. He dropped to the ground, grovelling before the oilpresser, swearing that he would do twice what the first devil had done if only his life would be spared and he not be branded. For a moment the oilpresser was perplexed but he soon realized what had happened. Not wanting to lose the opportunity for more gain, he asked angrily, 'And what will you do for me if I take pity on you?' 'I-I-I will d-do a great deal for you,' stammered the devil. 'In addition to the 100 bags of seeds which you now get, I shall provide you with 100 jars of fresh sesame oil.' The oilpresser was delighted. But he pretended he was grudgingly agreeing to this condition.

New Devil was thereafter branded and soon recovered. As for the other new devil, it is said that he is still providing the oilman with 100 bags of sesame seed and 100 jars of fresh sesame oil. The oilpresser is now not only the richest in the region but also in the country. His oil is particularly famous, as it is the purest sesame oil that one can buy anywhere.

How Birbal Saved his Life

The famous emperor Akbar, had a close friend called Birbal. Birbal had a sharp and intelligent mind. In addition, he was always ready with a witty remark. Akbar was so amused by his wit and his cleverness that he insisted Birbal stay at the palace. Wherever Akbar went, Birbal went too. There are consequently many stories made up about Birbal and this is one of them.....

*

The other courtiers in the palace resented Birbal's friendship with the emperor. 'Birbal does not come from a noble family as we all do,' they said. They were also jealous of his intelligence. They seldom had a kind word for him. They would have preferred the famous musician Tansen to occupy such a position of favour with the emperor. Akbar was annoyed at the dislike of his courtiers for his friend. He enjoyed Birbal's company and was determined to keep him, whatever the courtiers might say.

One day, Akbar is said to have called a special darbar. All the nobles of the land were invited to attend the meeting in the imperial audience-hall. It was a most impressive sight, as one by one the nobles arrived. Finally, there was the sound of drums and the emperor was announced. He walked down the length of the hall, greeting his nobles as he went. At the other end was the marble throne, on which he seated himself. The nobles were curious as to why he should have assembled them. What had happened? Was there going to be a war? Was he going to announce the marriage of his daughter? Had one of the princes rebelled? The herald called for silence. 'Dear nobles,' began the emperor, 'I have noticed that some of you are not pleased by the friends I have. There is one person in particular whom you do not like. You would rather that I sent him away and took one amongst you as a friend. No emperor can rule if his nobles are not satisfied with him. I have called you here today to say that if you wish it, I shall change my friends. But, since I am an emperor, I must also be just. Have I your permission to put my friends to a test? If the person who is selected is successful, I shall make him my friend, but if he fails, then don't you think it is fair that I need not accept him as a friend?'

The nobles agreed to this proposal. Everyone knew that Akbar was referring to Birbal, his friend, and to Tansen, whom the nobles wanted the emperor to adopt as his friend. Akbar continued, 'I believe that my friend Birbal is a man of superior intelligence. That is why I enjoy his company. Now there is one test that needs great intelligence and that is the ability to save oneself from death. I am going to condemn both Birbal and Tansen to death and whoever of the two can save himself will be my close friend.' This seemed fair enough to the nobles. But how was the emperor going to condemn them to death? 'My plan is as follows,' said the emperor. 'I have written two letters to the king of Burma, in which I have asked him to put the bearer to death. Birbal shall carry one letter and Tansen the other.'

On hearing this, Birbal was certain of his end. How could he ever manage to persuade the king of Burma not to kill him, when Akbar's letter demanded precisely this? Tansen himself was horrified at being involved in the argument and was furious with the nobles. He was a brilliant musician and wished to be left in peace. But it was too late. The emperor insisted that the two men should leave for Burma immediately.

They set out with heavy hearts. The journey was difficult enough without the constant fear that they were going to meet with death at the other end. They took a boat down the River Ganges. On arriving at the delta of the river, they moved to a larger ship which set sail for Burma. The sea was rough and the doomed men prayed that the storm would wreck the ship, and thereby end their agony. At last they arrived in the capital city, feeling tired and weak. But they had little time to lose. They bathed and changed into their best clothes since they wished to create a good impression on the king of Burma.

The king welcomed them with much enthusiasm. He believed at first that they had come as the envoys of the emperor of India. But when the letters were given to him and he had read their contents, he was extremely bewildered. He showed the letters to his minister who was equally baffled. The king and his minister retired into an ante-chamber to decide what they should do. Then they reappeared and the king questioned the two unfortunates. 'We wish to know why the emperor has acted in this fashion. We believe that there is some hidden motive behind all this. What is it?' Both Birbal and Tansen assured the king that there was no such motive. But the king refused to be convinced. 'You must have committed some terrible offence for the emperor not to allow even your bones or your ashes to remain in his kingdom.' Again the two insisted that they had committed no crime. Finally, the king announced that they would be executed but after eight days in prison. This, he thought, would enable them to think again and confess their crime.

Birbal and Tansen were put in a tiny cell, dark and musty, in the dungeons of the royal palace. It was a truly terrifying place. Tansen was the first to speak when they had been left alone. 'You know friend Birbal, that I have never questioned the superiority of your intelligence. As far as I am concerned, I was happy to know that the emperor had you as a friend. I am a musician and as long as I can sing, I am quite happy. I'm sorry if I ever had anything to do with the nobles at the court. Now that we are here, we must try to escape death. I am willing to try anything you may suggest.' Birbal was cheered by these words. He knew that Tansen was not really his rival. He thought for a long time.

Every day the minister would come to them and ask them if they were ready to confess and they would both reply that they had nothing to confess. But this gave Birbal an idea.

The morning of the ninth day was when they were to be executed. Outside the prison, a large space had been cleared where a block of stones had been placed. The executioner was busy sharpening his sword. The king arrived, accompanied by his minister. Then the two prisoners were brought out. But as they approached the executioner, they began to quarrel as to who should be executed first. Each of them seemed determined to be first. The quarrel was so harsh that if the guards had not separated them, they would have to come to blows. The king could not understand their behaviour. 'Why are you arguing as to who should be killed first?' he asked. 'Eventually you are both going to die. You still have time to confess your crimes, of course, if you wish to.'

Birbal now assumed a rather haughty air, and replied, 'My lord, the emperor Akbar had very special reasons for having us killed. He would not go to the extent of sending us all the way here if it were otherwise. But I'm afraid we cannot tell you anything more. Then the king said, 'Listen you obstinate ones. I am a Buddhist. For me, it would be a great crime to put two innocent people to death. That is why I am so anxious to know the nature of your crime so that I can satisfy my conscience. Of course, if you do not confess, then, I shall have to carry out the orders of my friend, the emperor of India.'

Birbal felt it was time now to try his trick, so he replied, 'Since you have been so kind to us, your Majesty, I shall tell you the reason for our emperor wishing to have us killed. As you know, he is the emperor of India. As you also know, when an emperor has such a large empire, he is greedy for more territory. Thus the emperor has for many years had his eye on Burma. He has been consulting priests, magicians and astrologers in an effort to discover how best he can conquer Burma. Some days ago, one of his astrologers advised him to send my friend Tansen and myself here, with letters such as those which we brought.' 'Yes, yes,' said the king impatiently. 'But why?' 'Have patience, my Lord,' replied Birbal gently. 'The reason is that the astrologer discovered that if we were killed, then immediately one of us would become the king of Burma in our next birth and the other would become minister to the king of Burma. So the emperor would not have to conquer Burma at all. His friends would be king and minister and it would therefore be easy for him to include Burma in his empire. So, soon after we are both executed we will be reborn, one as king and one as minister. And the moment this happens, you, O King, will die.'

'Indeed,' replied the king, deep in thought. 'So that was the reason. But tell me why both of you were quarrelling as to who should be killed first?' 'That is easy to explain, my Lord,' said Birbal. 'Whichever one of us is killed first is destined to be the king. We were fighting because we both wish to be king. The king laughed, and, turning to the executioner, said, 'There will be no execution today.' Then he addressed the two prisoners. 'I have two reasons for setting you free. Firstly, you are innocent of any crime; therefore I don't wish to incur the sin of putting two innocent men to death. Secondly, I wish to retain my kingdom longer than the emperor may think. I shall wait until you both die natural deaths!'

So Birbal and Tansen were freed. Having saved his own life and that of Tansen, Birbal now explained the whole truth to the king. The king, who had anyway suspected that their earlier story had been invented, was most amused by what Birbal narrated. He invited them to stay as royal guests for another week at the palace. Birbal entertained the king with his witty stories and Tansen enchanted the court with his music. The king of Burma was sorry to see them go. Birbal and Tansen, after some weeks of travelling, returned to the court of Akbar. The emperor was truly delighted to see them. The courtiers were amazed.

Another darbar was held. Akbar laughed heartily when he read the letter sent to him by the king of Burma. Even the nobles were amused. They readily granted the fact that Birbal was extremely intelligent and that Akbar was wise to have him as a close friend. 'I knew that he would find a way out,' said Akbar, 'else I would not have sent him. But now, my dear Birbal, you will have to help me draft a long letter in which I shall have to reassure my brother, the king of Burma. I don't want him to believe that I am really so greedy that I want his kingdom as well.'

The Throne of King Vikram

"Vikramaditya" is a title that was given to, or adopted by kings in the past. The title-holder supposedly possessed the valour of the sun. We do not know which king this story refers to, if at all it refers to any particular king.

We are told that a king called Vikramaditya ruled over a vast kingdom. He must have been a strong and powerful king who had fought many battles. But more importantly, Vikram was a wise king. He knew that a large army and fighting skills were not the real test of greatness. After all, any king with a large enough army and sufficient common sense would win victories against his enemies. True greatness lay in being able to keep the people happy and in inspiring their trust. Besides, a kingdom could not be called prosperous if only the king and his court were prosperous but if its people were so too. Above all, Vikram knew that people would be happy only if there was justice in the land. He therefore took great trouble to resolve each conflict that was brought to him. And in his final judgement, he would rarely give inhuman punishments.

This story is said to have taken place in the old city of Ujjain but we are not sure if this was so. Ujjain is said to have been a splendid city, with broad streets, tall and beautifully decorated buildings and many parks and pavilions. It was a wealthy city, because the merchants and traders would pass through it on their way to the ports of the west coast. Their caravans were laden with goods to send overseas. They brought finely woven cotton cloth, rich brocades, velvets, and embroidered silks; they brought spices and perfumes, talking parrots and prancing monkeys and a glittering display of their choicest gems, in colours both clear and deep.

But after some centuries, the wealth of Ujjain declined. The people became poor. The city walls and the houses started to crumble and fall into decay and the citizens did not have enough money to build again. Those that could, moved from the tottering city to new ones elsewhere. The old city, left in ruins, was covered through the years with earth and grass. Gradually the memory of it became dim, even among the people nearby. They knew that Vikram's palace was situated in the region but that was about all. . . . .

*

There were a number of villages in the vicinity and most of the people living in these villages reared cattle. They lived on the produce of the cows, selling the milk, butter and ghee. The ruins being deserted, the grass was allowed to grow wild and was therefore green and juicy most of the time. The young cowherds, the children of the villagers, would bring their cows to graze in the open, grassy spaces around the ruins. The cattle would be herded together in the village early in the morning. The children would then, shouting and prodding, direct them towards the open spaces. The cows would walk along, nibbling here and there at the grass, pausing for a moment to stare at the world around them with their large, black, shiny eyes, or else walk nimbly across to their companions, the bells round their necks tinkling with each movement. They would be out all day, wandering from pasture to pasture. As the sun began to set, the children would call out to the animals and again round them up and direct them home towards the village. And the cows would drift in, raising clouds of dust on the small village lanes as the twilight darkened the shadows.

The young cowherds who took the cows out to pasture had the entire day in which to play, to think, to sing and to invent stories. Some would take small flutes with them and would spend hours piping tunes. Others would invent stories and perhaps act them, in order to while away the time. Some who were bolder, would discuss ways and means of teasing the village girls. It was in the course of this type of amusement that one day, a group of cowherds found an unused part of the ruins of the old city in which to play. It was an open space which seemed to have stones arranged in an order. At one end was a raised mound which had the appearance of a throne. On either side of it were smaller stones.

The boys saw the shape of the stones and the arrangement and one of them shouted, 'It looks like a large audience-hall. I suppose that is the king's judgement-seat' (pointing to the raised mound). Another boy immediately invented a game to fit the situation. 'Let's play at having trials,' he suggested. 'I'll sit on the mound and be the judge. You invent quarrels and come to me and I'll pass judgement on all of you.' The idea caught on and the boys quickly split into groups and began to make up quarrels.

When they were ready, they would appear before the "judge". The quarrel was usually over pasture land and one of the boys would state his side of the story. Another boy would give his version of how his neighbour's cows came into his land and ate all the grass whilst his own cows had to go hungry. And then a third boy would add further complications to the story or would act as a witness to what one of the previous boys had said. And thus the "case" would grow and, in imitation of the real quarrels of their fathers, the boys would invent cases which had a ring of truth about them. As the game progressed amidst much laughter and amusement, the boy who was sitting on the judgement seat became very solemn and stern. He took the stories seriously and gave intelligent answers to the questions. His final judgements were extremely fair.

In the evening, the cows were once again rounded up and taken home. With the excitement of having discovered a new game, the boys related the day's events to their parents. At first the parents were also amused by the imagination of the boys. The elders of the village gathered in the evenings and heard the reports of the boys on the progress of their new game. But as the days went by, even the elders were surprised at the wisdom and maturity of the judgements made by the boy who sat on the mound and acted as the judge. It began to be whispered in the village that the opinions of the boy-judge showed greater fairness than even those of the village elders. Gradually, some of the villagers, in all seriousness, began to take their disputes and quarrels to the court of the young cowherds and listened with great attention to what the boy-judge had to say.

The villagers rightly felt that there was something strange about the whole business. The boy was, after all, only a cowherd and knew nothing about law and justice. In the village he behaved like any other cowherd, indulged in the same mischief as the others and was as often spanked by his father as were his playfellows. Yet the moment he went to the "court" in the ruins and sat on the mound, which by now was being called the "judgement seat", the boy changed completely. He became quiet and thoughtful and his words were so wise. Clearly there was something magical about the mound. All the disputes of the villagers were easily and happily settled, when taken to the cowherds' court.

The rumours and stories soon reached the ears of the king of the region. He was most interested and asked for details. When he heard the entire story from one of his courtiers, he was puzzled. But soon a thought struck him. 'If these are the ruins of Vikramaditya's city where the cowherds play,' he remarked to his courtiers, 'then surely the famous throne of Vikram may be buried under the mound on which the boy sits. His throne has been famous as the judgement seat of the wisest of kings.' The courtiers agreed that this was highly possible. The king then thought that it might solve all his problems if he could dig out the throne of Vikram and place it in his audience-chamber. If the throne could assist a cowherd to make wise decisions, then it would certainly be of the greatest help to him as the king of the realm.

The king's men arrived at the ruins and began to dig up the earth. Underneath was indeed an audience-room. But the most spectacular find was a magnificent black marble throne, supported by carvings in the shape of the mythical bird, the garuda. There could be no doubt that this was indeed the throne of Vikram.

The king was beside himself with excitement. The throne was carried immediately to his audience-room. It was cleaned, polished and placed in a position of honour. Prayers were said both in the palace and the city. The gods were requested to grant the prayer of the king, that he too might judge wisely and well, as did the Vikramaditya of earlier times. The heralds proclaimed that on a certain day the king would assemble with his court in the audience-room and that he would sit on the throne of Vikram and carry out the work of justice.

When the day arrived, there were crowds of people on the streets leading to the palace. Everyone was talking about the new era of justice that was now certain in the kingdom, with the help of King Vikram's throne. In the palace there was much bustle and scurry. There was music in the public rooms and in the gardens. Then the call to assembly was given and a procession was formed. The priests walked in front, chanting prayers and hymns. They were followed by the highest nobles of the land and finally, by the king himself. On the right, an attendant held up the royal umbrella of white silk embroidered with gold, from which hung tassels of pearls. On his left, another attendant fanned him with a large white flywhisk. Shouts of 'Glory to the King' rang though the air. The audience-hall was crowded with people eager to see the ceremony.

The king approached the throne. He paused a few steps away

from it, stood before it with folded hands, silently praying that his judgements may also be fair like those of the ancient king. He then moved close to the throne. Just as he was about to seat himself, one of the garudas seemed to stir its wings. A voice, clear and firm, addressed the king. 'Pause for a moment, O King. Before you seat yourself on this throne ask yourself whether you deserve this honour. Only the pure in heart, those that have been just and fair, can sit on this throne. Have you ever been unjust and tyrannical?' The king stopped still. A wave of anxiety swept through the people assembled in the hall. All was quiet. What would the king do? After what seemed to be many moments, the king stirred. 'I do not deserve to sit on this throne,' he stated in a voice full of sorrow. 'There have been times when I have been both unjust and tyrannical. I shall pray and fast for three days and then return to this hall.' So saying, he turned round and slowly left. All the assembled people left the hall quietly and silently. For the rest of the day, people talked in hushed whispers of this strange event.

After three days of prayer and meditation, the king felt that he had atoned for his past misdeeds and could now claim to be ready for the honour of sitting on Vikramaditya's throne. So once more the audience-hall was packed with people and the same ceremony was repeated. Once more, just as the king was about to sit on the throne, another garuda fluttered its wings and a voice asked, 'Is your heart pure now, O King? Are you sure that you deserve this honour?' Once again the king's courage failed him because he was suddenly made aware of all his faults and he knew that he was still not pure enough to claim the honour of sitting on Vikramaditya's throne. The same proclamation was made. The king would fast and pray for three days and then return to the audience-hall. The people turned back sadly and wondered what would happen.

Three days later the same story was repeated. This time another garuda spoke to the king and asked him the same

question, to which the king could only give the usual reply: no, he was not ready as yet.

The same thing happened on twenty-three occasions. Each time the king thought he was ready but each time he lost heart when the garuda put the question to him. Then came the last time. There was only one garuda left who had not yet spoken to the king. The people who had assembled looked worried and sad. They wondered if this time the king would be permitted to sit on the throne. The king himself had an anxious expression on his face and walked in a halting manner. Nobody knew what was going to happen. The nobles tried to encourage the king and said that, come what may, the king should definitely seat himself on the throne this time. He certainly deserved it by now. And, after all, it was only a carved stone bird that was speaking to him, they said. He should not take the matter seriously. But the king felt differently.

The ceremony was repeated with even greater solemnity. Finally, the king approached the throne. As was expected, the twenty-fourth garuda fluttered its wings and spoke. But this time his words were a little different. 'Do you not understand the purpose of our questioning?' he asked the king. 'Yes,' replied the king, speaking quietly and very slowly, 'I do understand. Only the boy, the cowherd was permitted to sit on the throne of Vikramaditya and he received the wisdom of the ancient king because he had never been unjust or tyrannical. He was worthy of the honour. Whereas I am not.' At these words there was a loud sound of rustling and movement. All the twenty-four garudas were flying back and taking up their original positions around the throne. Suddenly, to the great astonishment of the assembled crowds, the large black marble throne rose up in the air, borne aloft by the garudas who flew with it out of the audience-hall. There was silent amazement on the face of everyone present. Then the babble of voices broke out as everyone began to remark and comment on what had happened. The king strode across the empty space where the black marble throne of Vikram had stood a few moments earlier.' Silence!' he shouted. The people were fearful that the king would be angry at what had happened. But to their surprise, he was smiling.

'My noble lords and my subjects,' he addressed them. 'You have all witnessed the happenings of the last few weeks. You have all heard the questions I was repeatedly asked and my replies to them. I have thought for many days about these questions but I have only just really understood them and found the correct answer.' The assembly waited in expectation to hear the king's words. The king continued, 'The garudas did not permit me to seat myself on the throne of Vikramaditya. I was unworthy to do so because of my faults. But the true answer to their questions is: sitting on Vikram's throne alone would not make me a wise and just ruler. I should be wise and just wherever I may be, whether seated on the throne of Vikram or not. With this, the king left. The people realised that once more the judgement of Vikramaditya had been a wise one.

The Elephant and the Ant

There was a vast jungle which was ruled over by an elephant. The jungle had everything from tall grass to thorny bushes as well as thick, shady trees and many pools of water covered with water lilies. The deer would come to graze by the edge of the pools and would look curiously at the crocodiles half-hidden by the water lilies. In the thickets of the jungle, the big tigers and leopards would stalk their prey while the jackals crept up behind to try and pick up what might be left of the food. The vultures competed with the jackals. The cranes would come swooping down to pick at the ground for worms, competing with the geese and the chakravaka birds.

All the animals, big and small, accepted the elephant as their king and were ready to obey him. This made the elephant very proud and arrogant and instead of attending to the needs of the animals, he began to spend his time ordering them about. When some of the animals tried to tell him that this was not the right way to behave, he refused to listen to them. He began to believe that he was the wisest and the strongest of all the animals and could therefore treat them in any way he wanted.

The animals began to grumble mildly at first. Then slowly they grumbled more loudly and hoped that the elephant would hear them. But he was not interested in what they had to say. So one day, the animals gathered together and began to discuss what they could do with the elephant. Most of the animals were too frightened to say anything, in case someone went and told the elephant and he would then be really nasty to the animal who had spoken.

One small ant spoke up and said that it was willing to face the elephant and make him apologize for his bad behaviour. All the animals laughed at his offer and said it was impossible for a small ant to confront an elephant. But the ant insisted that it should be given a chance. It spoke with such passion that finally all the animals gathered there agreed. When the elephant heard that there had been a meeting and that an ant was coming to attack him, he laughed.

One day the elephant lay dreaming under a large, shady banyan tree. His lunch of sugarcane had put him in a pleasant mood. Slowly the ant crept up to where he lay, crawled into his trunk and little by little, climbed into his brain. The brain being a very delicate part of the body, any little change causes much pain. The elephant got up and in agony, rushed about trying somehow to stop the pain.

The animals were terrified as the elephant tore down the trees and swore to take revenge on whoever had caused his agony. In great fear, the animals confessed that it was the ant which had entered his brain. The elephant asked the ant to come out. It refused to do so unless the elephant agreed before all the animals to change his ways. The ant insisted that if the elephant wished to remain the king of the animals it would have to treat them as friends and not bully them. Above all, he was to promise that he would look after the welfare of all the animals.

The elephant agreed to everything. Slowly the ant came down from his brain and into his trunk and finally dropped onto the ground. The animals suddenly had great respect for the ant. They realized that even the smallest among them could tame the biggest. The elephant in particular, took care to keep to his bargain as he did not wish to suffer again.

The Ghost

There was much rejoicing in the house of the merchant, for his youngest son was to marry. His wife-to-be, a lovely young woman from the neighbouring town, was eagerly awaited by her in-laws. She travelled in a palanquin after the wedding, while her husband rode on ahead to welcome her home.

The palanquin-bearers became tired during the journey and rested under a bilva tree. The young bride stepped out of the palanquin to stretch her limbs. Just then the ghost who lived in the tree saw her and fell in love with her. The palanquin-bearers continued the journey and carried the bride to her new home. The ghost was left in the tree looking longingly after her.

A few weeks after his marriage, it was decided that the young man should go far away to the big town. He should establish a business and hopefully bring riches to his family. Sadly, the young man said good-bye to his wife and promised to return as soon as possible. The ghost had been watching all this and now decided to carry out his plan.

Some days later he took on the form of the young man and came to the house. Everyone was surprised at the early return. He explained that it was not the right time for his work and that he had decided to delay starting his business by a few months. So he was welcomed back and his young wife was especially happy.

The days passed into weeks, the weeks into months and the months into years. The household carried out its functions. Everything seemed to be going very well. Suddenly one day, the young man returned. He had been successful in his work and brought back the wealth he had earned.

You can imagine the shock that the family suffered. There were now two young men, each claiming to be the actual son of the parents and the husband of the young wife. Neither his parents nor his wife could decide as to which of the two was the genuine young man since they were identical in appearance.

The two young men fought, abused and accused each other of being a fraud. Everyone in the family was very upset. No one could understand how to solve this problem. So they all went to the head of the guild of merchants to ask his opinion.

The head of the guild listened carefully. After thinking for a while, he sent for a small leather bag and said to each of them that whichever of the two could turn himself into a tiny person and enter the bag was obviously the genuine young man. The real young man said that this was impossible. The ghost on the other hand laughed and immediately shrank and entered the bag. The head of the guild quickly tied the mouth of the bag which was then dropped into a well.

Thus was the family rid of the ghost. The young man was welcomed home, warmly.

The Crow and the Sparrow

One day a crow and a sparrow were searching for food in a garden. The sparrow found a grain of rice which it quickly ate and then looked for more. In the meanwhile, the crow found a small pearl and even though he could not eat it, he was delighted with it and started to play around with it. The sparrow seeing this, asked the crow for the pearl. But the crow did not want to give the pearl to the sparrow. So he picked up the pearl in his beak and flew to a tree nearby where he sat on a branch.

The sparrow was angry. It turned to the tree and said, 'Make the crow fly away.' But the tree would not do so.

The sparrow then asked the wood-cutter to cut down the tree. But the wood-cutter refused.

The sparrow asked the headman of the village to punish the wood-cutter. But the headman said that the wood-cutter did not deserve to be punished.

Then the sparrow went to the king and demanded that the headman be punished. But the king refused likewise.

So the sparrow tried the queen and said that she should show anger towards the king. But the queen saw no reason why she should be angry with the king.

The sparrow rushed to a mouse and asked the mouse to gnaw holes in the queen's clothes. The mouse said that the queen had not hurt it in any way so he would not do as asked.

The sparrow turned to a cat and said that the cat should eat the mouse. This, the cat refused to do.

The sparrow asked a dog to attack the cat. But the dog would not agree.

Then the sparrow said to a stick that it should beat the dog. But the stick remained where it was.

The sparrow wanted the fire to burn the stick. But the fire would not.

The sparrow turned to the sea and asked it to quench the fire. The sea refused.

The sparrow asked an elephant to drink up the sea. The elephant would not.

Then the sparrow became really angry and asked a mosquito to bite the elephant's ear so that the elephant would feel pain. And the mosquito agreed to do so.

The elephant quickly said, 'Wait, don't bite my ear. I'll drink up the sea.' And the sea said it would quench the fire. The fire said it would burn the stick. The stick said it would beat the dog. The dog agreed to attack the cat. The cat was willing to eat the mouse. The mouse was ready to gnaw the queen's clothes. The queen agreed to get angry with the king. The king said he would punish the headman of the village. The headman agreed to punish the wood-cutter. The wood-cutter was willing to cut down the tree. The tree was ready to make the crow fly away.

And the crow said angrily to the sparrow, 'What a big fuss you have made. This is not the way to ask for something. You can't always have it your way and threaten everyone. You are behaving like a bully and that is terrible. Unless you apologize for your behaviour, I will not give you the pearl.' So the sparrow said that it was sincerely sorry to have made such a fuss and to have been so nasty but it did think that the pearl was beautiful and would love to have it. Then the crow, out of friendship for the sparrow, relented and said, 'Here, take the pearl.'

The Grateful Snake

In a small village there lived a man, his wife and their daughter, Shobha. The land around was not fertile. It was difficult to grow crops so the families in the village kept cattle. There was grass nearby for the cattle to feed on and there was the forest where they could be taken to graze if they wanted more. The people of the village were poor.

When Shobha was eight years old, her mother died. After that she had to do all the household work herself. She would wake up early in the morning, milk the cow, sweep the house, take the cattle to feed on the grass and cook something at midday for her father. She would then take the cattle to the forest in the afternoon and bring them back when the sun was going down, cook some food for the evening and finish the household work before going to sleep. She would get very tired each day.

So one day she asked her father to marry again so that some of the work would be shared by a step-mother. But as it turned out, her father married a woman who expected Shobha to do *her* work as well. The young girl now had double the amount of work. And the work increased when two step-sisters were born.

Shobha had taken the cattle out to graze one day when suddenly a huge black snake appeared. She was terrified. But strangely enough, the snake asked for help. He said that he was being chased by snake-catchers who wanted to kill him for his skin. Shobha fearlessly placed the snake on her lap and covered it. When the snake-catchers came by and asked her if she had seen the snake, she said she hadn't.

After they left, the snake thanked her and within moments took on the shape of a god. He said he had been pleased by her

courage in sheltering him and would grant her any wish she might make. Shobha said she wanted a garden full of flowers and grass; a garden which would go with her wherever she went and where she could also graze her cows without having to walk long distances into the forest. This was immediately granted. The snake god also said that if ever she wanted help in future, she should call him.

A few days later, a young man was hunting in the forest and without realizing, entered the garden. He was delighted with its beauty. The cows got frightened by his horse and ran helter-skelter. When Shobha ran after them, the garden also moved along with her. The young man was amazed and asked her how this happened. So she told him her story. The young man, who was a prince from the neighbouring kingdom, often came to see Shobha in her garden and they became good friends. Eventually they were married. When Shobha moved to the prince's home, the garden went with her.

Shobha's step-mother was very jealous that she had married so well. She planned to kill Shobha, hoping that if she died, the prince would marry one of her daughters. So after a few weeks she persuaded her husband to visit his daughter. She prepared some sweets for her and put poison into them. The husband set out and when he was tired of walking, sat for a while under a large tree.

The same black snake lived in the tree. So whilst the man slept, he quietly removed the poison from the sweets. When the father arrived at the palace, Shobha was delighted to see him. She eagerly opened the pot containing the sweets and tasted them. They were delicious and enjoyed by everyone. Her father returned home happily. His wife was furious when she found that her plan had failed. She tried the same trick again and again but each time the snake would remove the poison.

When it was time for Shobha to give birth to a child, her step-mother invited her to come home as was the custom. So

Shobha gladly went. A son was born to her. After a few weeks she wanted to return to her husband but one day, her step-mother pushed her into the well. As she fell, Shobha called on the snake and was saved from drowning. Since this was not an ordinary well but had underground rooms leading off from it, the snake suggested that she would be safer for the time being if she lived in the well.

Meanwhile the step-mother dressed her daughter in Shobha's clothes and together with the newly-born, sent her to the prince. He could not recognize her but she said she had changed because of the birth of the child. Then he asked her what had happened to the garden but she could not explain why it was not there. The young prince became suspicious.

Every night there were hushed sounds in the palace because Shobha would creep in and play with her son. She missed not having him with her in the well. One night, the prince hid in the room and saw Shobha coming. He was overjoyed to see her and asked what had happened. She told him the story. He was so angry that he had the father banished, together with his wife and daughters. Shobha lived happily with her husband and her garden.

Banyan-Deer and his Herd

In a large forest there once dwelt a magnificent deer. He was the head of a herd of five hundred deer and was known as Banyan-deer. He was given this name because he was a tall animal with huge antlers which spread out like a tree. In the neighbouring forest there was another herd of deer and its leader was called Branch-deer. Both herds could have lived peacefully in the forest but for the king of Banares.

This king was very fond of eating meat and enjoyed venison in particular. So everyday he would gather the people of the town and insist that they accompany him on his hunt. The townspeople became rather fed up of this routine as it interfered with their daily work. They decided that a method would have to be found whereby the king could get his venison easily without disrupting their work.

They made a decision to capture the deer. They built a huge stockade with a gate. Near it they planted some thick, juicy grass and diverted a stream of water. All the townspeople came to the forest. When the two herds of deer began to graze on the delicious grass, they made a tremendous noise by shaking the bushes and beating the trees with their sticks. Thus surrounded, the deer from the two herds were in a panic and got pushed into the stockade. Once they were in, the townspeople shut the gate. Having captured the herds, they went to the king and told him that he could now easily shoot whichever deer he wanted without going on an elaborate hunt.

The king was delighted and went to look at the deer. He saw the two large deer who were the heads of the herds—Banyan-deer and Branch-deer. They were so handsome that the king vowed to them that he would never kill them. But as for the rest, there was great sorrow. Everyday, more than one deer got killed since those who were wounded, died of their injuries later. The herds were being rapidly reduced. Banyan-deer and Branch-deer sat together to seriously think the matter over.

Eventually they decided that it would be better if each day, turn by turn, a deer from one herd and then from the other, went to the gate and offered itself for the king's table. The plan was put into action. The days went by. The two herds managed to survive without too much damage, except that it was always a sad parting when the deer whose turn it was to go, said goodbye to the others.

Now one day it came to the turn of a pregnant doe. She was deeply upset since she was about to deliver a fawn. She went to the head of her herd, Branch-deer, begging him to give her time so that her baby might be born. She asked that someone else take her turn and that she go after the fawn had been born. But Branch-deer insisted that the rules must be observed and if her turn had come there was nothing he could do about it.

So in desperation she went to Banyan-deer and begged him to help. He was more sympathetic and told her to go home and that he would take care of her turn. After she had gone, he went to the gate himself and offered his life. The king was astonished.

Banyan-deer explained what the matter was. The king had never come across anyone so full of love and concern for others. So he immediately ordered that the lives of Banyan-deer and of the pregnant doe were to be spared. Banyan-deer said that that still did not take away from the sorrow of the herds when every morning one among them had to go to its death. So the king promised not to ask for any more deer from the herd.

At this, Banyan-deer said, 'What about all the other deer in the other forests where you will hunt?' The king promised to spare their lives too. Then Banyan-deer raised the question of other four-footed animals. These too, the king promised to spare. So Banyan-deer was emboldened enough to ask about the lives of the flocks of birds and eventually even the fish in the water. All these the king promised not to kill. And the animals of the forests and the rivers went their way peacefully.

After some time, the doe gave birth to a lovely fawn. Together with other young deer he would go to play with Banyan-deer. But as they grew up, the younger deer became lazy. Instead of searching for patches of good grass in the forest, they saw the crops of the farmers nearby and starting grazing there. The fresh grain was greener and tastier than the grass. The farmers tried to scare them but they kept coming back. The farmers did not know how to stop them since they were forbidden from killing the deer. So they got together and went to the king to ask his advice. The king said that he could not go back on his word. The farmers were helpless.

When Banyan-deer got to hear of this he was angry with his herd. He called them together and forbade them from eating the crops. He also made them promise that they would stop other deer from doing the same. He explained that the king had given them his word that they could live without being killed but that this did not mean that they could destroy the food and labour of others. He sent a message to the farmers that henceforth no deer would eat their crop. And no deer did.

Baz Bahadur and Rupamati

The city of Mandu is perched on top of a hill. It is fun to climb up slowly, getting the feel of the countryside around. It is particularly magnificent after the monsoon, with its dark grandeur in the midst of the richness of the surrounding fields and the many hues of green from the trees and shrubs.

A few centuries back, there was a wild jungle in the vicinity where the emperors of India would go hunting. In those times, lions roamed this jungle. When camps were set up on the hillside, lions would wander through them at night. But now there are no lions left. Most have been shot by man.

Along the crest of the hill lie the pavilions and palaces and the mosques and tombs of Mandu. Built of stone and decorated with painted plaster, they were once resplendent buildings. Today they look dark and on occasion, even sullen, having known better times. Once their halls echoed to the sounds of music and of girls dancing; to the footfalls of the horses returning from the hunt or from a battle; to the call to prayer from its many mosques; to the sounds of the bustling traders who came long distances and continued their travel to far away places, halting and exchanging goods and gossip at Mandu; or to the even softer sounds of people in quiet conversation.

Today one walks from building to building to the echoes of the past. There is the deep *baoli*, or well, with its underground rooms and passages where people moved in the heat of the summer to keep cool. The large tanks and ponds had elaborate platforms and walkways for there would be evenings of singing and dancing. On the extreme edge of the hill, overlooking the plain, is the palace of Rupamati and this has its own story.

Afghan Kings ruled from the city of Mandu. One among them, Baz Bahadur, is specially remembered by the people of Malwa because he was different from the others. He had little time for battles and for court matters. What he valued most was his love for Rupamati and the music which they heard together. Their story is told in the ballads and songs of Malwa to this day.

*

One day Baz Bahadur was out hunting a lion. The chase took him deep into the forest. He lost track of the lion and whilst he was trying to find his way back to Mandu, he suddenly heard the sound of a woman singing. He followed the voice and came to a spot in the forest where he saw the woman who was singing so beautifully. This was Rupamati.

Baz Bahadur came often to the forest to see her and to hear her sing. He loved her deeply and wanted her to come to Mandu with him. At first she refused. Finally, she said that she would do so if he could take her river up to Mandu. This was the River Rewa, which flowed through the plains near Mandu and on whose banks she had grown up. What she asked for was the impossible, for no one can take a river up a hill.

Baz Bahadur thought of every possible solution. He even prayed to the Rewa to help him. Eventually he was told that there was a tamarisk tree on the hill and beneath this tree was a spring from which the water flowed into the Rewa. But there were many tamarisk trees. After much searching, Baz Bahadur found the right one with a spring and this became the pool which he called the Rewa-kund. Thus he had found a source and the water flowing from the pool eventually led to the river. In this way he claimed that he had brought the Rewa up to Mandu. Rupamati came joyfully to live in the palace which was built for her beside her beloved river.

Years passed and Baz Bahadur and Rupamati were wrapped

102

in their love for each other and in the music which they composed and heard. Meanwhile, the Mughal emperor Akbar was anxious to control Mandu and rule over Malwa. So he sent his army, commanded by his redoubtable general Adham Khan. Mandu was besieged and a battle began. Baz Bahadur tried to defend his city but failed and in the midst of battle, he was cut off from Mandu. Having lost the battle, he fled to a place near Rupamati's home, thinking that perhaps Rupamati might be able to join him there.

But Adham Khan moved swiftly into Mandu. Rupamati's fame had spread even to the Mughal court and he was anxious to see her and hear her sing. So he gave orders that she was not to be allowed to get away. Having secured her in her palace, he sent a request to her that he wished to spend some time with her. Rupamati was terrified, as she knew what this meant. The victor seldom treated those close to his defeated opponent with any mercy. She also knew that Adham Khan would try to lure Baz Bahadur to Mandu by using her presence as a bait.

To begin with, she kept making excuses and tried not to see Adham Khan but he became more and more insistent. Eventually, she agreed. She dressed with care that evening, almost like a bride. The room was sprinkled with perfume and flowers. She said she wanted to rest for a short while before Adham Khan came to see her and so the maids withdrew.

After a while Adham Khan arrived, resplendent in his courtly dress, and entered her palace. He greeted her and asked if he could sit on the divan beside her. There was no reply from her. She did not stir. She had poisoned herself and had died, so anxious was she not to fall into the hands of the victor. She also feared that Baz Bahadur would try and see her secretly in Mandu and in the bargain, get killed. As it happened, Baz Bahadur was indeed killed soon after.

*

Songs about Rupamati continue to be sung in Malwa. And stories such as this one continue to be told. They may only partly be true but the memories of Baz Bahadur and Rupamati remain popular. If you go to Mandu on a clear day and stand in Rupamati's pavilion, you can see the Rewa in the far, far, distance. And if you stay quietly and long enough you might perhaps, in your mind's eye, even catch a glimpse of Rupamati and Baz Bahadur, standing on the same balconies and gazing out at the river which had bound them together.